Cesare P

# AMONG WOMEN ONLY
Translated from the Italian
by D. D. Paige

sceptre

Translated from the Italian *Tra Donne Sole*

First published in Great Britain in 1953 by Peter Owen Ltd

English translation © Peter Owen Ltd 1953

Sceptre edition, 1990

Sceptre is an imprint of Hodder and Stoughton Paperbacks, a division of Hodder and Stoughton Ltd

**British Library C.I.P.**

Pavese, Cesare, *1908–1950*
   Among women only.
   I. Title   II. Tra donne sole.
   *English*
   853′.912[F]

ISBN 0-340-51479-5

Printed and bound in Great Britain for Hodder and Stoughton Paperbacks, a division of Hodder and Stoughton Ltd, Mill Road, Dunton Green, Sevenoaks, Kent TN13 2YA. (Editorial Office: 47 Bedford Square, London WC1B 3DP) by Richard Clay Ltd, Bungay, Suffolk. Photoset by Rowland Phototypesetting Ltd, Bury St Edmunds, Suffolk.

# CESARE PAVESE

The author, the son of a judiciary official in Turin, was born in 1908 on a farm in Piedmont. He was educated in Turin, where he took his literature degree with a thesis on Walt Whitman. He later became a school-master.

In 1930 he began to contribute essays on American literature to *La Cultura*, of which he became editor in 1934. Concurrently he began a series of translations of books by English and American writers (Defoe, Dickens, Joyce, Melville, Stein and Faulkner), whose work exerted considerable influence not only on his own narrative style, but also on that of other Italian novelists.

In 1935 he was arrested for anti-fascist activities and sentenced to preventive detention at the lonely sea-shore prison of Brancaleone (Calabria). This formed the basis of THE POLITICAL PRISONER. Between 1936 and 1940 nine of his books were published in Italy, and these included novels, short stories, poetry and essays.

His books have been filmed and dramatised, and translated into many languages. He committed suicide in 1950.

# ONE

I arrived in Turin with the last January snow just like a juggler or a nougat peddler. I remembered it was carnival time only when I saw the stands and the bright points of the carbide lamps under the porticoes, but as it was not yet dark I walked from the station to the hotel, squinting out from under the arches and over the heads of the people. The sharp air bit my legs and tired as I was I huddled in my fur and loitered in front of the shop windows, letting the people bump into me. I thought of how the days were getting longer now and of how before long a bit of sun would dry up the sludge and usher in the spring.

That was how I saw Turin again, in the half-light under the porticoes. When I entered the hotel I didn't think of anything but having a hot bath and of lying down and of a long night. Especially since I had to stay in Turin for a while.

I telephoned no one and no one knew I was stopping at that hotel. Not even a bouquet of flowers awaited me. While I wandered about my room, the maid who was preparing my bath chattered away, bent over the tub. A man, a valet, would not do such things. I told her to go, that I would be all right alone. The girl babbled something, standing in front of me, her hands shaking. Then I asked her where she came from. She reddened quickly and replied that she was Venetian. 'You can tell from the accent,' I said. 'And I'm from Turin. You'd like to go back home, I suppose?'

She nodded brightly.

'Then remember that I've just come home', I said; 'don't spoil the pleasure for me.'

'I beg your pardon,' she said. 'May I go?'

Alone in the warm water, I closed my eyes which ached from too much talking that wasn't worth the effort. The more I convince myself that talking is no use the more need I have to talk. Especially among women. But my tiredness and a slight feverishness soon dissolved in the water and I thought of the last time I had been in Turin, during the war, the day after a bombing raid: all the pipes were burst, no bath. I thought with pleasure: as long as you can have a bath, living is worth the effort.

A bath and a cigarette. While I smoked, my hand dangling above the surface of the water, I contrasted the protracted bathing which now lulled me with the exciting days I had seen, with the tumult of countless words, with my impatient desires, with the projects which I had always realised: this evening they all had come down to that tub and that pleasant warmth. Had I been ambitious? I saw the ambitious faces file before me: pale, marked, convulsed faces – did one of them ever relax for a peaceful hour? Under the drive of ambition you do not relax even when you are dying. It seemed to me I had never relaxed for a moment. Perhaps twenty years before, when I was still a little girl playing in the streets and waiting with beating heart for the season of confetti, booths and masks, perhaps then I might have been able to relax. But in those years the carnival meant only merry-go-rounds, nougat and cardboard noses. Later there was the desire to go out, to see Turin, to run through it; there were the first escapades in the alleys with Carlotta and other girls when, hearts beating, we felt ourselves being followed for the first time: all this innocence had come to an end. Strange. The evening of the Thursday before Lent when father was growing worse just before dying. I cried with anger and I hated him, thinking of the holiday I was losing. Only mother understood me that evening, teased me and told me to get out from under her feet and go and cry in the courtyard with Carlotta. But I was crying because the idea of father's dying terrified me and prevented me from abandoning myself to the carnival.

The telephone rang. I didn't move from the tub because I was happy with my cigarette. I thought that it was probably in that distant evening that I really learned for the first time that if I wanted to do anything, to get something out of life, I should tie myself to no one, depend upon no one, as I had been tied to that tiresome father. And I had succeeded, and now my sole pleasure was to dissolve myself in warm water and not answer the telephone.

It began to ring again after a bit, seemingly irritated. I got out of the water, but I didn't answer it. I dried myself slowly, seated in the bathrobe, and was rubbing face-cream around my mouth when a knock came. 'Who is it?'

'A note for madame.'

'I said I'm not in.'

'The gentleman insists.'

I got up and turned the key. The impertinent Venetian handed me the note. I glanced at it and said: 'I don't want to see him. He can come back tomorrow.'

'Madame is not going down?'

My face felt plastered, I couldn't even manage a frown. I said: 'I'm not going down. I want tea. Tell him tomorrow at noon.'

When I was alone, I lifted the receiver and put it beside the telephone but immediately they answered from the office. The voice rasped helplessly on the table, like a fish out of water. Then I shouted something into the telephone, I had to tell them who I was, that I wanted to sleep. They wished me good-night.

Half an hour later the girl had not yet returned. This sort of thing can only happen in Turin, I thought. I did something I had never done before, as though I were a silly girl. I slipped into my dressing-gown and half-opened the door.

In the not over-elaborate corridor a number of persons –

servants, clients, my impertinent maid – crowded before a door. Someone exclaimed something in a low voice.

Then the door opened wide, and slowly and very carefully two white shirts carried out a stretcher. Everyone fell silent and gave way. On the stretcher lay a girl with a swollen face and disordered hair, shoeless but wearing an evening gown of blue tulle. Though her lips and eyelids were motionless, you could imagine she had had a lively expression on her face. Instinctively I glanced below the stretcher to see if blood was dripping. I looked at the faces – they were the usual ones, one with pursed lips, another with a cynical smile. I caught the eye of my maid – she was running behind the stretcher. There broke in upon the low murmurs of the group, which included a woman in fur who wrung her hands, the voice of a doctor; he had come out of the door wiping his hands, saying that it was all over, that they should get out of the way.

The stretcher disappeared down the stairs, I heard some one say: 'Easy there!' I looked at my maid again. She had already run to a chair at the end of the corridor and returned with the tea-tray.

'She was taken ill, poor girl!' she said entering the room. But her eyes were shining and she couldn't contain herself. She told me everything. The girl had entered the hotel in the morning – she had come alone from a party, a dance. She had locked herself in her room; she hadn't moved all day. Some one had telephoned; people were looking for her; a policeman had opened the door. The girl was on the bed, dying.

The maid continued: 'Poisoning herself at carnival time, what a shame! And her people are rich . . . They have a beautiful house in Piazza d'Armi. It'll be a miracle if she lives . . .'

I told her that I wanted more water for the tea. And not to loiter on the stairs this time.

But that night I didn't sleep as I had hoped I would and tossing about in bed I could have kicked myself for having stuck my nose into the corridor.

# TWO

The next day they brought me a bouquet of flowers, the first narcissi. I smiled thinking that I had never received flowers in Turin. But they hadn't come from Turin. The order had come from that owl Maurizio who had thought of surprising me on my arrival. Instead the thing had gone wrong. Such things can happen in Rome, too, I thought. I imagined Maurizio, unhappy, wandering aimlessly down the Via Veneto after the goodbyes and, between the last coffee and the first aperitif, filling out the form for wiring flowers.

I wondered if the girl yesterday had had flowers in her room. Are there people who surround themselves with flowers before dying? Perhaps it's a way to keep up one's courage. The maid went to get a vase and while she helped me arrange the narcissi she told me that there was nothing in the papers of the attempted suicide. 'Who knows how much they paid to keep it quiet? They took her to a private nursing home . . . Last night they made an investigation. There must be a man mixed up in it . . . There ought to be a law for getting a girl . . .'

I said that a girl who spends evenings at parties and instead of going home goes to a hotel ought to be considered capable of looking out for herself.

'Yes,' she said, indignant, 'it's the mothers' fault. Why don't they go along with their daughters?'

'Mothers?' I said. 'These girls have always been with their mothers, they grew up on velvet, they've seen the world behind plate glass. Then when they have to get out of a mess, they don't know how and they get tangled up worse.'

After which Mariuccia laughed, as if to say that she knew how to get out of a mess. I sent her out and got dressed. In the street it was cold and clear; during the night it had rained and now the sun entered under the arcades. Turin seemed like a new city, a city just built and the people who ran about seemed to be there almost accidentally as though giving it the last touches. I walked under the buildings in the centre, looking at the large shops which waited for their first customers. None of those show windows and signs was humble and familiar, as I remembered them, nor the cafés, nor the cashiers, nor the faces. Only the sun slanting down and the moist air had not changed.

And no one strolled along; everybody seemed to be busy. The streets weren't for living in, but only to escape by. To think that when I used to pass those central avenues with my big box on my arm they seemed to me a kingdom of carefree people on holiday, in a way in which I then pictured seaside resorts. When one wants a thing one sees it everywhere. And all this that I had wanted and got only meant suffering and barking my shins. What did that stupid girl who took veronal want? I asked myself. A man mixed up in it . . . Girls are fools. My Venetian was right.

I entered the hotel and saw Morelli's lean, unexpected face before me. I had forgotten him and his note.

'How did you find me?' I said laughing.

'It's nothing. I waited.'

'All night?'

'All winter.'

'That means you must have plenty of time.'

I had always seen this man in a bathing suit on the beaches frequented by Romans. He had hair on his thin chest, a grey, almost white hair. But now his silk tie and light-coloured vest had changed him completely.

'You know you're young, Morelli?' I said.

He bowed and invited me to lunch.

'Didn't they tell you last night I don't go out?'

'Let's eat here then,' he said.

I don't find them at all displeasing, these people who joke and amuse you without ever laughing. They make you feel timid and consequently you feel safe with them.

'I accept,' I told him. 'On condition you tell me something amusing. How's the carnival going?'

When we sat down he didn't talk about the carnival. He didn't even talk about himself. Without smiling he told a little story about a Turin salon – he gave the name: nobility – where it happened that certain important gentlemen while waiting for the mistress of the house stripped down to their undershorts and then sat down in the armchairs smoking and talking. The hostess, astonished, was sure that this antic was a new fashion, a trial of spirit, and for a long time she stayed there joking with her guests.

'You see, Clelia,' Morelli said, 'Turin is an old city. Anywhere else such a lark would have been perpetrated by boys, students, young men who had just opened their first offices or just got their first government appointments. Here, however, elderly people, *commendatori* and colonels, play such tricks. It's a lively city . . .'

Still expressionless he leaned forward murmuring: 'That bald-headed chap there is one of them . . .'

'He won't take me for the countess?' I said lightly. 'I'm from Turin too.'

'Oh, you're not in the same set; he knows that.'

It wasn't wholly a compliment. I imagined his grey-haired chest. 'Did you undress too?' I asked.

'My dear Clelia, if you want to be introduced in that salon . . .'

'What would another woman do there?'

'She could teach the countess striptease . . . Who do you know in Turin?'

'Busybody . . . The only bouquet I got here came from Rome.'

'They're waiting for you in Rome?'

I shrugged my shoulders. He was clever, Morelli, and he knew Maurizio. He also knew that while I liked to play around I paid my own way.

'I'm free,' I said. 'The only obligation I recognise is the one you owe a son or daughter. And unfortunately I have no children.'

'You could be my daughter . . . perhaps that makes me too old?'

'It's me that's too old.'

Finally he opened up and smiled with those lively grey eyes. Without moving his mouth in a smile he became full of high spirits, looked me over with appreciation. I knew that too. He wasn't the type to run after a chit.

'You know everything about this hotel,' I said; 'tell me about yesterday's scandal. Do you know the girl?'

He looked me over again and shook his head.

'I know her father,' he said, 'a hard man. Strong-willed. A sort of buffalo. He makes motorcycles and goes about his factory in overalls.'

'I saw her mother there.'

'I don't know her mother. Good people. But the daughter is crazy.'

'Completely?'

Morelli darkened. 'When they try once, they try again.'

'What do people say?'

'I don't know,' he said. 'I don't listen to such conversations. They're like the conversations during the war. Speculations . . . It could have been anything. A man could have been behind it; or it might have been a sudden caprice or a resentment against somebody or something. But there's only one real cause.'

He touched his temple with a finger. He smiled again with his eyes. He held his hand on the oranges and said: 'I've always seen you eat fruit, Clelia. That's real youth. Leave flowers to the Romans.'

The bald fellow of the story muttered something to the waiter, threw down his napkin and went off, fat and solemn. He bowed to us. I laughed; Morelli, expressionless, nodded.

'Man is the only animal,' he observed, 'who labours to dress himself.'

When the coffee came he had not yet asked me what I was doing in Turin. Probably he knew already and there was no need to tell him. But he didn't even ask how long I was staying. I like this in people. Live and let live.

'Do you want to go out this evening?' he asked. 'Turin by night.'

'First I've got to have a look at Turin by day. Let me get myself settled. You staying here in the hotel?'

'Why not come to my place?'

He really had to say that. I let the proposal drop as though it were absurd. I told him to call for me at nine.

He repeated: 'I can put you up at my place.'

'Don't be foolish,' I said; 'we're not children. I'll come and pay you a visit one day.'

That afternoon I went out on my own, and in the evening he took me to a ball.

# THREE

When I returned in the evening, Morelli, who was waiting for me, remarked that I had gone out in a cloth coat and not a fur. I had him come up and while I was getting ready I asked him if he spent his days in the hotel.

'I spend my nights at home,' he said.

'Really?' I was talking into the mirror, with my back to him. 'Don't you ever spend any time on your estate?'

'Oh yes, whenever I happen to pass over it in the train on the way to Genoa. My wife lives there. Nobody like women for certain sacrifices.'

'Married ones too?' I murmured.

I felt that he was laughing.

'Not only them,' he sighed. 'It hurts me, Clelia, that you should go around in an overall supervising whitewashers . . . However, I don't like that situation in the Via Po. What do you think you're going to sell there?'

'Turin is really the most gossipy old concierge.'

'Cities grow old like women . . .'

'For me it's only thirty. Oh well, thirty-four . . . But I didn't choose the Via Po. They chose it in Rome.'

'Obviously.'

We left. I was glad that Morelli, who understood everything, hadn't understood why I went out that day in a cloth coat. I was thinking about it when we got into the taxi and I thought about it after. I believe that in the hubbub of the ball when the cherry brandy, the kümmel and the introductions had reduced me to feeling irritable and unhappy, I told him.

Instead of going to the Via Po I had gone to the hairdresser. A little hairdresser two steps from the hotel, and while she was drying my hair I heard the sharp voice of the manicurist behind the glass partition tell how she was awakened that morning by the smell of milk on the gasburner. 'What a mess! Even the cat couldn't stand it. Tonight I'll have to clean the burner.' That was enough for me to see a kitchen, an unmade bed, dirty panes on the balcony door, a dark staircase seemingly carved out of the walls. Leaving the hairdresser I thought only of the old courtyard, and I went back into the hotel, left the fur coat and took the other. I really had to go back to the Via della Basilica, and perhaps someone could recognise me; I didn't want to seem to put on airs.

I had gone there; I had first walked about the district. I knew the houses, I knew the stores. I pretended to stop and look in the shop windows, but really I was hesitating; it seemed impossible that I had been a child in such crannies, and at the same time, with something like fear, I felt I was no longer myself. The quarter was much dirtier than I recalled. Under the portico of the little square I saw the shop of the old herbalist; now there was a thin little man, but the sacks of seeds and bunches of herbs were the same. During summer afternoons that shop used to give off a pungent smell of countryside and spices. Further down, the bombs had destroyed an alley. Who knows what's become of Carlotta, the girls, Slim? Or of Pia's children? If the bombs had flattened the whole district it would have been easier to walk about with my memories. I went down a forbidden alley, I passed by the tiled doorways of the brothels. How many times we had spent running by those doorways! The afternoon that I had stared at a soldier who came out with a dark look . . . what had got into me? And by the time I was old enough to dare to mention such things (and that district made me less afraid than angry and disgusted) I was going to the shop in another section of town and I had friends and I knew all about it because I was working.

I arrived in the Via della Basilica and didn't have the courage. I passed in front of the courtyard, I caught a glimpse of the shallow vaulting of a second storey bedroom and of balconies. I was already in the Via Milano. Impossible to return. The mattress-maker looked at me from his doorway.

I told Morelli something of all this at the height of the party when it was nearly morning and one drank and talked, all played out, in order to hold on a bit longer. I said: 'Look, Morelli . . . All these people dancing and getting drunk are well-born. They've had butlers, wet nurses, maids. They've had country holidays, favours. Nice work! Do you think any of them would have been able to start from nothing – from a courtyard the size of a grave – and get to this party?'

And Morelli patted my arm and said: 'Buck up. We've got here. If necessary we'll even get home.'

'It's easy,' I said, 'for the wives and daughters of wealthy families to dress the way they're dressed. All they have to do is ask. They don't even have to sleep around. Give you my word, I prefer to dress real whores. At least they know what work is.'

'Do whores still dress?' Morelli said.

We had eaten and danced. We had met many people. Morelli always had someone at his shoulder who was saying loudly: 'Be seeing you.' I recognised some faces and names: they were people who had been in our fitting room in Rome. I recognised some gowns: a countess wore one with a peplum, which we had designed and which I myself had sent several days before. A small woman in ruffles even gave me a little smile; her escort turned round; I recognised him too; they had been married the year before in Rome. He bowed deeply and gravely in recognition – he was a tall, blond diplomat – then he was jerked away: I suppose his wife recalled him to propriety by reminding him that I was only the dressmaker. That was when my blood began to boil. Then came a collection for the blind: a man in a dinner-jacket and a red paper hat made a comic speech about the blind and deaf and two blindfolded women ran around the room grabbing hold of men who, after paying, could kiss them. Morelli paid. Then the orchestra began playing again and some groups began to make an uproar, singing and chasing one another. Morelli returned to the table with a large woman in rose lamé with the belly of a fish; a young man and a cool young woman who had just finished dancing suddenly dropped on the divan. The man immediately jumped up.

'My friend Clelia Oitana,' Morelli was saying. The large woman sat down fanning herself and looked at me. The other in a low-cut, clinging violet gown had already examined me and smiled at Morelli who lit her cigarette.

I don't recall the first part of the conversation. I was watching the younger woman's smile. She had an air of having always known me, of mocking both Morelli and me although she was only watching the smoke curl up from her cigarette. The other woman laughed and prattled nonsense. The young man asked me to dance. We danced. His name was Fefé. He told me something about Rome, tried to glue himself to me and squeeze me, and asked me if Morelli was really my squire. I replied that I wasn't a horse. Then laughing he squeezed me tighter. He must have drunk more than I.

When we came back, there remained only the large woman who was still fanning herself. Morelli was moving about the room. Fish-belly sent the young man, who was bored, off to find something, then she patted me on the knee with a feeble little hand, her eyes were malicious. My blood boiled again.

'You were in the hotel,' she whispered, 'when poor Rosetta Mola was taken ill last night?'

'Oh you know her? How is she?' I asked immediately.

'She's out of danger, I hear.' She shook her head, sighing. 'Tell me, did she really sleep in the hotel? What girls! She was locked in all day? Was she really alone?'

Her fat, bright eyes bored in like two needles. She was trying to control herself but didn't succeed.

'Imagine! We saw her the night of the dance. She seemed

calm . . . Such distinguished people. She danced a great
deal . . .'

I saw Morelli approaching.

'Listen. Did you see her afterwards? They say she was
still in her evening gown.'

I brought out something: that I had not seen anything. A
furtiveness in the old woman's tone induced me to hold back.
Besides I felt spiteful. Everybody came up – Morelli, the
brunette in violet, the unpleasant Fefé. But the old woman
opening wide her large sharp eyes said: 'I was really hoping
that you had seen her . . . I know her parents . . . What a
shame! To want to kill oneself. What a day! . . . One thing's
certain, she didn't say prayers in that bed.'

The brunette smoked curled up on the divan and looking
at us mockingly said to me: 'Adele sees sex everywhere.'
She blew out a puff of smoke. 'But it's no longer the fashion
. . . Only servants or dressmakers' assistants want to kill
themselves after a night of love . . .'

'A night and a day,' said Fefé.

'Nonsense. Three months wouldn't have been enough . . .
As far as I'm concerned, she was drunk and mistook the
dosage . . .'

'Probable,' said Morelli. 'Rather, it's certain.' He bent
towards the fat woman. Instead of taking her by the arm, he
touched her shoulder and they went off, he joking, she
bouncing.

The brunette turned around, exhaling a cloud of smoke,
glanced at me and praised my silk-print gown. She said it was
easier to dress in Rome. 'It's different there. Designs are
more exclusive. Did you make it yourself?'

She asked this with her dissatisfied and mocking air.

'I don't have time to make my dresses,' I snapped. 'I'm
always busy.'

'Do you see any people?' she asked. 'Do you see so-and-so?
Do you see such-and-such?' There was no end to the names.

'So-and-so and such-and-such,' I said, 'don't pay by day the debts they contract at night. And as for *her,*' I went on, 'when too many bills become due she disappears to Capri . . .'

'Marvellous!' the brunette shouted. 'What nice people!'

They called to her from the crowd; someone had arrived; she got up, brushed the cigarette ash from the front of her gown and hurried over.

I remained alone with Fefé who looked at me dumbly. I said: 'You're thirsty, young man. Why don't you go and make your rounds?'

He had explained before that his method of drinking was to make the rounds of all the tables, recognise somebody at each one and accept a drink. He had said, grinning: 'You get all kinds of drinks. However . . . When you dance you shake up a cocktail.'

I sent him off. Morelli returned and gave me a thin smile.

'Like the women?' he asked.

Then it struck me that the party didn't mean much to me and I began to tell him what I really felt.

# FOUR

But before he left me that evening Morelli lectured me. He said that I was prejudiced, that I had only one prejudice, but a big one: I believed that working to get ahead, or even working just to get by, was as valuable as the qualities – some admittedly stupid – of well-born people. He said that when I talked enviously of certain fortunes I had an air of taking it out on the pleasure of living. 'At bottom, Clelia,' he said, 'you wouldn't think it right to win the football pools.'

'Why not?' I said.

'But it's the same as being well-born. It's a bit of luck, the person's every bit as privileged . . .'

I didn't reply, I was tired, I pulled him by the arm.

Morelli said: 'Is there really such a big difference between doing nothing because you're too rich and doing nothing because you're too poor?'

'But when you win out by yourself . . .'

'There you are,' Morelli said. 'Win out. A sporting programme.' He scarcely moved his mouth. 'Sport means Spartan training – all that sort of thing – in short, renunciation and quick death. What's against stopping along the road and enjoying the day? If one can? Does one always have to have suffered and come out of a hole?'

I kept quiet and pulled him by the arm.

'You hate other people's pleasures, Clelia, and that's a fact. It's wrong. You hate yourself. And to think you were born with such talents! Be happy, forget that grudge of yours. Other people's pleasure is yours too . . .'

The next day I went to the Via Po without announcing myself or telephoning the contractors. They didn't know I had already arrived in Turin; I wanted to get an unrehearsed impression of what had been done and how it had been done. When I entered the wide street and saw the hill in the background spotted with snow and the church of the Gran Madre, I remembered that it was carnival time. Here, too, stands with nougat, horns, masks and coloured streamers filled the spaces under the arches of the porticoes. It was early morning but the people were swarming toward the square at the end of the street where the booths were.

The street was much wider than I remembered. Along one side the war had opened a frightful hole, gutting three or four large buildings. It seemed like a yard, a cavity of earth and stones where a couple of tufts of grass grew: you thought of a cemetery. Our shop, spotted white with lime and without its show-window or even its steel grille, stood at the empty yard, under construction.

Two plasterers wearing white paper caps were seated on the floor. One was dissolving whitewash in a bucket and the other washing his hands in a lime-caked can. Without the least discomposure they watched me enter. The second man had a cigarette stuck above his ear.

'The supervisor's never here at this hour,' they told me.

'When does he come?'

'Not before evening. He's working at Madonna di Campagna.'

I asked if they were the whole gang. They looked at my hips with interest, not raising their eyes very much.

I stamped my foot. 'Which of you is the boss?'

'He was here a minute ago,' said the first.

'He's probably in the square.' He lowered his eyes and continued stirring the whitewash. 'Go get Becuccio,' he said to the other.

Becuccio arrived, a young man in a heavy sweater and army trousers. He understood at once what was up, he was wide awake. He shouted at the two to finish the floor. He took me around by the stairs and explained the work that had been done. He said that they had lost time because they had been waiting several days for the electricians and that it was useless to put in the shelves when they didn't know how the wiring was to be done. The supervisor wanted it concealed in the walls; the utility company advised them to have it visible and accessible. As he talked I inspected him: he was thick-set, curly-headed and when he smiled showed his teeth. He wore a leather wristband.

'Where can one telephone the supervisor?'

'I'll do it,' he said immediately.

I was wearing my cloth coat, not the fur. We crossed the Via Po. He took me into a café where the cashier recognised him with a shining smile. When he got a reply he handed me the receiver. The heavy snarling voice of the supervisor changed immediately when I told him who I was. He complained that a letter he had sent to Rome hadn't been answered; he was full of excuses; he even brought up the Building Authority; I cut him short and told him to get here in half an hour. Becuccio smiled and held the door open.

I spent the whole day in the smell of lime. I examined the plans and correspondence which the supervisor shuffled out of a frayed leather briefcase. Becuccio got us a couple of boxes and set up a little office on the first floor. I made note of the work that had to be done, allocated the money for the bills due, talked a long time with the man from the utility company. Over a month had been lost.

'As long as the carnival lasts . . .' the supervisor said.

I said curtly that we wanted the shop ready at the end of the month.

We looked over the bills again. I had first questioned Becuccio and knew how things stood. And I had come to an agreement with the man from the utility company. The supervisor had to agree to get the job done.

Between discussions I walked through the empty rooms

where the whitewashers were now working on their feet. Another pair showed up in the area-way. I went up and down a cold staircase without a railing, cluttered with brooms and cans; the smell of lime – a sharp mountain smell – turned my head so that I almost thought this was my own building. From an empty window on the mezzanine I caught a glimpse of the Via Po, crowded and festive at that moment. It was nearly dusk. I remembered the tiny window in my first workroom from which you looked out in the evening as you were making the last stitches, impatient for closing time to come and then going out happy. 'The world is large,' I said to myself aloud, without really knowing why. Becuccio was waiting discreetly in the shadows.

I was hungry. I was tired from last night's party and Morelli was probably waiting for me at the hotel.

Without leaving instructions for the next day, I left. I spent half an hour among the crowds. I didn't walk towards the Piazza Vittorio Veneto, noisy with orchestras and merry-go-rounds. I had always liked to sniff about the carnival from alleys and half-shadows. I recalled many holidays in Rome, many buried and forgotten things, many follies. Out of all of which remained only Maurizio, crazy Maurizio, and a certain peace and balance. No, there remained also the fact that I could wander idly about like this, my own mistress, and could stop when I liked and arrange what I liked for the next day.

As I was walking I began to think of that evening seventeen years before, when I had left Turin, having persuaded myself that a person can love another more than himself; yet at bottom I really knew quite well that all I wanted was to leave Turin and step out into the world, and I seized that excuse, that pretext, for taking the step. And there was Guido, blissfully ignorant, believing that he was carrying me off to support me – and all the while I was running the affair from the beginning. I let him argue, let him try and finally let him do it. I even helped him, I went out before closing time to keep him company. That would be my, according to Morelli, ill-will and ill-humour. For three months I had laughed and made Guido laugh: had it been the least use? He wasn't even capable of leaving me. You just can't love someone else more than yourself. If you can't save yourself, nobody can.

But – and here Morelli was not wrong when he had spoken of the football pools – I nevertheless had to be thankful for those days. Wherever he was, whether dead or alive, I owed my fortune to Guido and he didn't even know it. I had laughed at his extravagant words, at his way of kneeling on the carpet and thanking me for being everything to him and for liking him, and I said: 'I don't do it on purpose.' Once he said: 'One does one's biggest favours without ever knowing it.'

'You don't deserve them,' I said.

'No one deserves anything,' he had replied. Seventeen years. I had at least another seventeen coming to me. I was no longer young and I knew what a man – even the best – was worth. I ended up under the porticoes and looked at the shop windows.

# FIVE

In the evening Morelli took me to a salon. I was astonished at the number of young people there: they always say Turin is a city of old people. Of course, the young men and girls formed a group apart from the adults, as if they were so many children, while we grown-ups, seated around a sofa, were listening to an irritable old lady with a ribbon round her throat and a velvet mantle tell some story I don't recall about Mirafiori and a carriage. Everyone in front of the old lady was quiet; someone smoked, almost as though on the sly. When people entered, her irritable little voice stopped to let them exchange the customary greetings and at the first pause took up the story. Morelli, his legs crossed, listened very attentively and another gentleman stared at the rug with a wrinkled forehead. But little by little I realised that you didn't have to pay attention to the old lady. No one thought of answering her. Half-turned on her chair some woman would be whispering away, while another would rise and speak across the room to others.

It was a beautiful room, with glass chandeliers and a Venetian floor which you felt under your feet right through the rug. A fire was burning on the hearth to one side of the sofa. I sat motionless, my eyes exploring the walls, the upholstery, the lamps, the varnished tables covered with sweet-dishes. There was a bit too much, but the room was planned that way, crammed like a jewel box; and curtains covered the windows.

Someone touched my shoulder and whispered my name

and I saw the hostess's daughter in front of me, tall and gay. We exchanged several words and then she asked me if I knew so-and-so and such-and-such.

I replied no in a low voice.

'We know you come from Rome,' she shouted laughing into an unexpected silence, 'but yesterday evening you met a girl-friend of mine. You can't say you didn't!'

'Who?'

Of course I had understood immediately: she meant one of those two at the ball. But being taken in hand the way she took me annoys me.

'You must have met Fefé at least?'

'I'm surprised he remembers. He was drunk as a carter.'

Which reply struck her fancy. I had to get up and follow her to the circle of young people near the entrance to the room. She told me their names: Pupé, Carletto, Teresina. They shook hands, either bored or very very serious and waited for someone to speak. The flood of words with which the blonde had torn me from the sofa did not keep me from feeling an intruder even here; nevertheless, as I had known for quite a while, in such cases there is always somebody else who feels worse. I cursed Morelli and felt my heart drop; I saw the life of Rome, the ball, my face in the mirror that morning. I consoled myself by thinking of the Via della Basilica and that I could be as independent as I liked and that, after all, these were people whom I might never have seen.

The blonde was looking at us dumbly and, it seemed to me, with disappointment. Then she said: 'Come on, somebody say something.' For all her twenty years and so much desire to laugh and be happy, she hadn't brought out much. But I didn't know Mariella's tenacity – she was the granddaughter of the old lady on the sofa. She looked around and exclaimed: 'Where's Loris? Somebody find Loris. I want Loris right away.' Someone went to look for Loris. The others began to talk, one kneeling against a chair, another seated; a young man with a beard held the floor and defended an absent friend against the girls – a certain Pegi, who had shoveled snow on the avenues that winter: out of eccentricity, the girls said; to engage himself, the young man said.

'Engage himself ' – what's he mean by that? I thought, as Loris arrived with lowered head. He wore a black bow tie and was a painter. The suspicion flitted across my mind that he owed his importance among those people wholly to his bow tie and heavy eyebrows. He had a sullen look, like a bull.

He smiled briefly. Mariella dropped on to a chair and said to us: 'Come on now, let's discuss the costumes.'

When I had finally understood what it was all about – a girl beside me screaming louder than all the rest set herself to explaining it – I pretended ignorance and smiled impassively. Mariella and the others were all talking.

'Oh no, without costumes and a stage you just *can't*!'

'You're all a bunch of hams . . . If you can't, *Carmen*'s preferable.'

'It would be better to organise a costume ball.'

'The poetic word must resound in empty space.'

'But had any of you *read* it?'

I glanced to the other side of the room where the irascible old lady talked and talked to her circle, and the men in the light of the fireplace stared at the carpet; the women moved restlessly and the first cups of tea had appeared in their hands.

Loris was saying slowly: 'We don't want to repeat the traditional theatre. We're not so civilised. What we want to do is isolate the bare word – strip down to the naked word. Well then, how do we do it? We can't do it without any *mise-en-scène* at all, for that, too, is a *mise-en-scène*. Even here in this room, between these four walls, dressed as we are, we form a part of a *mise-en-scène*. What we've got to do is have scenery that consumes itself and pegs the senses of the audience to the bare word alone. The staging must destroy the surroundings. Any given surrounding is a *mise-en-scène*. Even the light . . .'

'Then let's give it in the dark,' a girl screamed. While Loris continued that way, Mariella got up and went off to supervise the serving and then she called the girls. I remained with the few people left, including Loris, who now fell silent and was smiling disgustedly.

'There's something in that idea of giving it in the dark,' a young man said.

We looked at Loris who was staring at the floor.

'Ridiculous!' said a small woman seated by us wrapped in a slipper-satin gown worth more than a lot of words. 'One goes to the theatre to *see*. Are you or aren't you giving a show?' She had libidinous eyes which laughed at the boys.

The painter did not think much of her remarks and changing expression he said rudely that he didn't want tea but a drink. At the same time the cups arrived among us and Mariella placed a bottle of cognac on the mantelpiece. She asked me if we had come to any conclusion.

'Was I supposed to come to a conclusion?' I said. 'I have no ideas.'

Mariella shouted: 'But you've got to help us. You know all about styles.'

A general movement around the sofa indicated that something was happening. Everyone got up and moved back and Mariella ran over. The old lady was leaving. I didn't hear what she said, but a pretty maid took her thin arm and the old lady jabbed her cane on the floor, looked round tiredly out of bright eyes and as the others bowed the two went out slowly, with hobbling steps.

'Grandmother wants us to keep the doors open so she can hear in bed,' said Mariella, returning fresher than ever. 'She wants to hear the records, the conversation, the people. She's absolutely in love with our friends . . .'

At the first chance I cornered Morelli and asked him what his idea was in bringing me here. 'Out of temper already?' he said.

'Less than you; you've had a good dose of the old lady . . . However . . .'

'Don't speak badly of her,' Morelli observed. 'One sees precious few like Donna Clementina. Her sort died out some time ago. D'you know she's a concierge's daughter, became an actress, a dancer, several times a mistress and that of the three sons she had by the old count one ran off to America and the other is an archbishop? To say nothing of the daughters . . .'

'Poor old thing. Why doesn't she retire to the country?'

'Because she's full of life. Because she likes to run her house. You ought to get to know her, Clelia.'

'She's so old . . . frightens one.'

'That's a good reason for knowing her. If you're afraid of old people you're afraid to live.'

'I thought you brought me to meet those others . . .'

Morelli looked at the seated groups in the room and the couples chattering at the other end.

He darkened and muttered: 'Drinking already?'

# SIX

They didn't talk about the play for the rest of the evening. I saw Loris's black bow tie fluttering about, but I drifted around alone and Mariella must have understood for she took me among a group of women, including her mother, who were talking about fashions. Did she think she was doing me a favour? She returned to the subject of her friend at the ball, said that she, Mariella, would have liked to have gone but that she felt too young. Just then the stretcher and the tulle gown came to mind.

'Oh, you could have come,' said the little woman in slipper-satin; 'it was quite proper. I know of people who even change the place of a party right in the middle of it, just for fun.'

'Oh, it was just a properly chaperoned family affair, I suppose?' Mariella said sarcastically.

'Absolutely,' someone else said.

'More likely there were wandering hands in the dark,' Mariella concluded viciously, looking around.

The women smiled, scandalised and happy. Mariella was by no means a fool; she was presiding as hostess and she had been born in such talk. I wondered if she would have known how to get along if she had begun at the bottom as her grandmother had. Morelli's remarks returned to my mind and I stopped thinking like that.

Then we began to talk about him, Morelli, and his life. By mentioning Rome and well-known Roman villas and certain important names which I included deliberately, I quieted the most snobbish of the group. I gave them to understand that

Morelli was at home in some of the best houses and that Rome is the only city you don't have to leave. Everybody else comes to Rome. Mariella clapped her hands and said she was having such a good time and that some day she would visit Rome. Someone mentioned the Holy Year.

'Those poor things,' Mariella said suddenly. 'What are they doing? Shall we go and listen to them?'

Thus our circle broke up and various groups merged and separated around the bow tie of Loris, who, assailed by three or four girls, was holding forth. Just for a lark he and the others had drunk up all the cognac and now they were bawling like bulls on I don't know what subject – whether you can really be yourself in life or whether you have to act. I was surprised when I heard a thin girl with bangs, thick lips and a cigarette shout the name of the brunette I had met at the ball – Momina. 'Momina said so. Momina said so,' she repeated. Just as Mariella ran up to the group with all those distinguished people gathered around, an uncertain voice rose: 'When you're really making love, that's when you take off the mask. You strip yourself naked.' While Mariella looked after the refreshments, I turned to Morelli. He had a satisfied air and was watching as though he wore a monocle. I caught his eye with a smile and when he had come up I asked in a whisper why they didn't send the tightest ones into the garden. 'They'd be in the open and not give any trouble.'

'You can't,' he said. 'The indecencies must be maintained only in the salon; the ladies and parents have to hear them. More regular that way.'

I asked him who these horrible boys and girls were. He told me their names, letting me understand that they weren't all respectable people, that youth had corrupted and was continuing to corrupt them – 'I'm not talking about social rank, dammit, but who, after the war – or before it too, for that matter – understands anything at all about these things?'

'It used to be that one could mix among all sorts of people; but we were aware then of our identities, we knew who we were. But these here don't know who they are any more, or what they want,' he continued. 'They don't even have a good time. They don't know how to make conversation: they shout. They have all the vices of the old without the experience . . .'

I thought of the girl in the tulle gown and was about to mention her and ask if he had heard anything more about her. I didn't however; I knew that he was obstinate about such matters, that with all his moods he had hair on his belly and was grey and grown old. You're as old as my father, I thought. You know so many things and you know nothing. He kept quiet at least and let us do everything . . .

Morelli was now in the crowd, arguing. He was telling the bearded chap that they should learn how to treat women instead of talking stupidities and should learn how to live and stop being children; and all the while the young man, of course, was trying to convince him and get him to agree that all of us are not our real selves in daily life but only acting rôles. I had never seen Morelli so annoyed. The women were amused.

I caught Mariella as she went by, smiling very self-possessedly at a preoccupied gentleman, and I took her aside and said that we – that is, I – wanted to say good-night and thank her for the evening. She was surprised and said that she wanted to see me again, that she wanted to talk to me about many things, to convince me to do something for them and that Momina had already told her how nice I was.

'She didn't come this evening,' I said just to say something.

Mariella brightened and excused Momina. She said that Momina had telephoned saying she wasn't sure and that she wanted to visit the Molas.

'You know? . . .' – raising her eyes and lowering her voice.

'Yes,' I said. 'How is Rosetta?'

Then Mariella coloured and, flustered, said that if I knew Rosetta we should have to talk about it; poor thing, her parents didn't understand her and made life impossible for her, she was strong and sensitive, she absolutely needed to live, to have things, she was more mature than her years and she, Mariella, was afraid that now their friendship would not survive that terrible experience.

'But how is she?'

'Yes, yes, she's recovered, but she doesn't want to see us, she doesn't want to see anyone. She only asks for Momina and won't see anyone else . . .'

'That's nothing,' I said, 'provided she gets better.'

'Of course, but I'm afraid she hates me . . .'

I looked at her. She appeared upset.

'It's the nausea after the veronal,' I said. 'When someone's sick in the stomach she doesn't want to see people . . .'

'But she sees Momina,' Mariella shot back immediately; 'it makes me angry.'

I thought: You've still to grow up, my dear; if I were in your place I'd know how to control myself better.

I said: 'Rosetta didn't drink veronal just to spite you.' I said this with a smile and indicated by my expression that I was taking leave. Mariella smiled and held out her hand.

I said good-night to the nearest people. I left Morelli in his circle with the bow tie and the girls and went away. Outside it was drizzling and I took a tram on the avenue.

# SEVEN

Two days went by and during the morning of the third Mariella telephoned me. I hadn't seen anyone since that evening and had spent the whole time in the Via Po. The girl's voice laughed, insisted, panted with volubility. She wanted me to see her friends, to see them for her sake and help them out. Would I be able to visit her that afternoon for tea? Or better, could we stop a moment in Loris's studio?

'That way we'll encourage them,' she said. 'If you knew how nice they are . . .'

She picked me up at the Via Po; she was wearing a fur jacket in cossack style. The house was on the other side of the Po. We went under the porticoes around the square and Mariella drew away from the holiday stands without even glancing at them. I was thinking that though severed from Rome by only a few days I had already found responsibilities in Turin and the company of people who had always lived there. Even Maurizio, after that morning of my arrival, had sent no more narcissi.

Chattering along, Mariella told me many things about life in Turin and about the shops. For having seen them always as a customer she knew them well. To judge a shop by its show-window is difficult for a person who has never dressed one. However, Mariella understood them. She told me that her grandmother was still the terror of the dressmakers.

We arrived at the top of a dirty stairway that made a disagreeable impression on me. I should have preferred to have continued talking. Mariella rang.

All painters' studios are alike. They have the disorder you find in certain shops, but studied and done on purpose. You don't know when it is that they work, they always seem to have the curtains drawn against the light. We found Loris on the unmade bed – without his bow tie this time – and the girl with bangs opened the door. She had on a coat which had lost most of its fur and she looked at Mariella with displeasure. She was smoking. Loris also was smoking, a pipe; and both seemed put out of temper by our arrival. Mariella laughed warmly and said: 'Where's my stool?' Loris didn't move from the bed.

We sat down with forced gaiety. Mariella began her prattling, asked news, was astonished, went to the window. Loris, black and taciturn, scarcely replied. The thin girl, whose name was Nènè, examined me. She was a strange heavy-lipped girl of about twenty-eight. She smoked with impatient gestures and bit her nails. She smiled nicely, like a child, but her abrupt manner was annoying. It was clear that she considered Mariella a fool.

As it happened, I expected what followed. They began to talk about their own doings and people I didn't know. There was the story of a painting which had been sold before it was finished but then the painter became aware that it was already perfectly finished as it stood and he didn't want to touch it any more and the client wanted it really finished and the painter wouldn't hear of it and refused to hand it over. Nènè got heated, indignant and agitated, she bit on her cigarette and interrupted Mariella, taking the words out of her mouth. I understand people's talking shop; but of all those you hear arguing in restaurants and cafés there's none can beat painters. I could understand if they talked about brushes, colours, turpentine – the things they use – but no, these people talk obscurely because they like to and sometimes no one knows what certain words mean and there's always somebody else who suddenly begins to argue, says no, that it means such and such and everything's upsidedown. They are words like those in the newspapers when they write about paintings. I expected that Nènè too would overdo it. But no. She talked rapidly and angrily, but did not lose that childish air: she explained to Mariella that one never stops a painting too soon. Loris remained silent, sucking his pipe. Mariella, who cared nothing about pictures, suddenly came out with: why didn't we discuss the play? Loris turned over on the bed. Nènè looked unpleasantly at both of us. She was aware of it herself and exploded with laughter. It struck me that she laughed in dialect, as counter-girls laugh, as I sometimes do myself.

Nènè said: 'But it's all up in the air now. After what's happened to Rosetta one can't put on a suicide . . .'

'Nonsense!' Mariella shouted. 'Nobody'd think twice about it.'

Nènè looked at us again, provocatively and happy.

'That's all woman's stuff,' Loris said, contemptuous. 'It might interest the bourgeois householder, but as for me . . . Anyhow we've got to deal with the Martelli females and the others putting up the cash. I don't know what Rosetta did, but this very real fantasy of hers strikes me as pretty good. By her mere act she concretised an abstract artistic situation into warm life. I don't care where the personal fact has its origin . . . But it would be really too good if she did it from the suggestion in the play itself . . . Anyhow, the Martellis have backed out.'

'What's all this have to do with it?' Mariella said. 'Art's another thing . . .'

'Are you sure?' Loris argued. 'It's another way of looking at the thing, if you like; but it's not another thing. As for me, I'd like to dramatize the germ of the dramatic suggestion. I'm sure it would be fantastic . . . a collage of theatre news . . . to consider these dresses that you wear, this room, this bed, like the properties of Mary Magdalene . . . An existentialist theatre . . . Is that right?'

He looked at me, really at me, from his bed, from under

his heavy eyebrows. I can't stand these nasty-clever people and I was ready to tell him off when Nènè jumped up, fresh: 'If Rosetta had really died, one could put it on. *Un hommage à Rosette* . . .'

Mariella said: 'Who's not in favour of putting it on?'

'Momina,' the other replied. 'The Martellis, the president, Carla and Mizi. They were Momina's friends . . .'

'The fool should have died, it would have been better . . .' Mariella cried.

I'm used to hearing all the scandals and gossip of Rome in our shop, but this bickering between friends because a third one didn't succeed in killing herself struck me. I was on the point of believing that the acting had already begun and that everything going on was make-believe, as in a theatre, as Loris wanted. Having arrived in Turin I had entered the scene and now I too had a part to play. It's carnival, I thought to myself. You'll find out that in Turin they play these tricks every year.

'As for me,' Loris said biting his pipe, 'agree among your-selves.'

I studied Nènè's bangs, her heavy lips, her faded coat. People live in strange ways. Listening to them talk about their work and the right they had to sell it unfinished I understood that they were not so much defending the money as their arrogance. I wanted to say to her: 'My dear, you never know where the next meal's coming from and yet you put on such airs. Where do you sleep at night? Does someone keep you? Mariella, who doesn't paint, is well-born and well-dressed.'

They began to argue about the play again and said that there wasn't enough time to find another, and all right, they wouldn't do anything for this year.

'That fool!' Mariella said.

'Let's read a single act, without action or stage,' Nènè said.

And then Loris jumped up and said: 'All right. Only don't come looking for me.'

I glanced again at a certain unframed picture against the wall under the window. It seemed dirty and unfinished: from the moment I had arrived I had been asking myself what it was. I didn't want anyone to see me looking at it because I didn't want Mariella to say: 'Come on, show her your pictures.' But that mess of violet and blackish colours distracted me; I didn't want to look at it and yet I always returned to it, I thought to myself that it was just like the room and Loris's face.

I said something. I asked when they had planned to give the play. 'Who knows,' Nènè said. 'Nobody's put a penny into it yet.'

'Don't you have someone who'll pay?'

'People who pay,' Mariella said nastily, 'try to impose their tastes on us . . .'

Loris said: 'I'd be delighted if someone would impose taste on me . . . Trouble is you never find anyone who has taste. They don't know what they want . . .'

Mariella laughed satisfied into her fur.

Nènè said excitedly: 'There are too many Martellis and too many Mizis in this. Too many hysterical females . . . Momina . . .'

'She overdoes everything,' Mariella said.

'Momina knows what she wants. Let her do what she likes.'

'And who's coming to hear us?' said Mariella, annoyed. 'Who'll do the acting? The hysterical females?'

'Acting is out. We'll read only.'

'Nonsense,' Loris said. 'We wanted to colour an ambience . . .'

They continued for a bit. It was clear that the painter only wanted to daub some scenery to earn a little money. And that Mariella wanted to be an actress. Only Nènè seemed without pretence, but I felt that there was something at the bottom of her interest too.

Then Momina arrived.

# EIGHT

She entered with that discontented, dominating attitude of hers. Her gloves alone were worth more than the whole studio. Nènè, opening the door to her, seemed like a servant. Everybody said hello smiling.

'Why, you visit everyone,' Momina said on seeing me.

'That's not difficult in Turin,' I replied.

She moved here and there going up very close to the pictures and I saw that she was nearsighted. All the better. I watched Mariella closely.

'Put on the lights,' Momina said; 'don't you see it's night?'

When the lights came on, the window disappeared and the painting became a puddle of flayed faces.

'Everybody's dropping out,' Nènè said. 'I'm dropping out too. One loses time over a lot of stupid excuses and we still don't know what to do. Clara's right, we ought to act it in the dark like a broadcast . . .'

Momina smiled in her dissatisfied way. She didn't answer Nènè, and instead told Loris that she had spoken to so-and-so who had said such-and-such, and Loris, sitting on the bed and holding his ankle grunted something; Mariella launched into their conversation and they chattered and laughed and Nènè said: 'Oh, my God,' and they didn't talk any more about the theatre. Now Momina took over the conversation and told a story about a certain Gegè, from Piovà, who entered the bar of a large hotel where he ran into a girl who had been his childhood playmate, and he went up to her: 'Hello.'

'Hello.'

'They tell me you've developed,' and slipping his hand down the front of her dress he took out a tit and they both laughed together with Filippo the bartender and the onlookers. Momina and Nènè laughed; Mariella looked disgusted; Loris jumped up from the bed saying, 'It's true. She has magnificent tits.'

'Slander,' Mariella said. 'Vanna's not like that.'

'They're not magnificent?' Loris said.

They went on like that and Momina skipped from one subject to another, looked at me out of the corners of her eyes in her searching way, constantly asked my opinion, wanted to enchant me. I was glad that they didn't return to the subject of the play. Only Mariella was ill at ease, you saw that Momina had taken over her place. Momina was younger than I, but not by much: she dressed very well, a grey suit under her beaver coat, her skin was massaged, her face fresh; she took advantage of her nearsightedness by passing it off as distraction. I recalled her violet dress the night of the ball and I looked at her ring-finger which was empty.

'We're leaving,' Mariella said suddenly.

Momina told us to wait for her, that she had her car below. We got into a green Topolino: I had expected something better. Mariella wanted to sit in the back. Lighting up a cigarette Momina explained: 'This is all my husband allows me.'

'Ah,' I said.

'I live alone,' Momina observed, putting the car into gear. 'Better for him, better for me.'

I wanted to get out at the Via Po to have a last look at things for the day; Momina said: 'Spend the evening with me.'

Mariella, in the back seat, said nothing. We dropped her at the gate on her avenue. To let her get out, we got out too, pulling the backs of the seats forward. At the last minute she began talking about the play again, about Mary Magdalene, complained about Momina, about us, accused us of having put a spoke in the wheel. Momina replied coldly, then they flew at one another while I looked at the shrubbery. Now they were quiet. 'I'll tell you all about it tomorrow,' Momina said to her. We got into the car.

She took me to the centre, she didn't say anything about Mariella. Instead she talked about Nènè and said that she made such beautiful sculptures. 'I can't understand why she wastes her time with that Loris,' she smiled. 'She's so intelligent. A woman who's worth more than the man who touches her is damned unfortunate.'

I asked her to take me to the Via Po.

When I came out from under the portico and approached the car, Momina was smoking and looking through the windscreen into the dark. She reached over and opened the door for me.

We went to the Piazza San Carlo for an aperitif. We sat down at the back of a new gilded café, the entrance to which was still encumbered with trestles and rubbish. An elegant place. Momina turned back her coat and looked at me. 'Now you know all my friends,' she said. 'From Rome to Turin is a nice jump. It must be pleasant to work as you do.'

I thought: What's she after? A job?

'. . . Don't be alarmed,' she went on, 'the circle here in Turin is small . . . I'm not asking you for advice. You have good taste but I'm satisfied with my own dressmaker . . . It's just that it's a pleasure to talk with someone who lives a different sort of life.'

We talked a bit about Turin and Rome – she squinting at me all the while through the smoke – about how you can't find apartments, about the new café we were in; she said she had never been in Rome but that she had been in Paris and asked if I didn't think I ought to go to Paris because of my work: I absolutely had to: travelling on account of work was the only kind of travelling possible, and why should I be satisfied with Turin?

Then I said I had been sent here. 'I was born in Turin.'

She was born in Turin too, she told me, but she grew up

in Switzerland and got married in Florence. 'They brought me up a lady,' she said. 'But what's the good of being a lady if you can't catch a train tomorrow for London or Spain or wherever you like?'

I opened my mouth, but she said that after the war only working people like myself could afford the luxury of travelling.

'When you work you don't have time,' I said.

She observed calmly: 'It's not worth working just to come to Turin.'

I believed I understood her, and I told her that I hadn't been in Turin for nearly twenty years and had come to see my home too.

'But I understand you're all alone.'

'I mean the house I lived in, the district . . .'

She looked at me with that discontented smile. 'I don't understand these things,' she said coldly. 'You probably have nothing to do with the girl born in Turin. Your family . . .'

'All dead.'

'. . . If they weren't dead, they'd make you laugh now. What could you have in common with them any more?'

She was so cold and distant that my face flushed and I didn't know what to say. I felt a fool. Then it occurred to me that, after all, it was a sort of compliment. She looked at me mockingly, as if she had understood what had just run through my mind.

'Now don't tell me, the way someone I know would, that it's pleasant being born in a courtyard . . .'

I said that it was pleasant thinking about the courtyard and contrasting it with now.

'I knew it,' she laughed. 'Living is such a foolish thing that we hold to it even through the foolishness of being born.'

No question about it, she knew how to talk. She looked round at the gilding, the mirrors, the prints on the walls. 'This café,' she said, 'was put up by a man like yourself, strong-willed . . .'

She succeeded in making me smile. I thought: Are you clever because you went to Paris . . . or did you go to Paris because you were clever?

But she said abruptly: 'Did you enjoy yourself at the ball the other evening?'

'Was that a ball?' I murmured, disillusioned. 'I wasn't aware.'

'They say it's carnival time,' Momina remarked ironically in a low voice, laughing; 'these things happen.'

'And pretty Mariella,' I asked, 'why doesn't she go to these balls?'

'She's already told you that?' Momina smiled. 'Why you're real friends already.'

'Well, she hasn't asked me to remake a dress for her yet . . .'

'She will, she will,' Momina said. 'We're all like that in Turin . . .'

# NINE

I'm a fool. In the evening I was sorry to have spoken badly
of Mariella after she had defended that girl Vanna in Loris's
studio. The bitterness remained in my mouth. Of course, I
knew that they were only words, that these people – all of
them, including Morelli – lived like cats, always ready to
scratch and snatch; but anyhow I was sorry and said to myself:
'Here I am just like them.' It didn't last long, however, and
when Momina asked me what I was doing in the evening, I
agreed to keep her company. We went to the hotel to eat
and naturally Morelli popped up and came over to our table
to talk, not showing any surprise at seeing us together.
Midway through the meal the telephone call I expected from
Rome came through. For a couple of minutes in the booth I
discussed the Via Po, made projects and breathed the old air.
On returning to the dining-room, Morelli and Momina told me
to forget all that, they'd made up their minds to have a good
time, we'd go out somewhere together and afterwards go to
Morelli's apartment.

   That evening Morelli wanted to drive. He took us to the
wine market where he tried to get us drunk as men do with
inexperienced girls, but it turned out that he drank more than
we did. And then, as though we were playing some sort of
game, we made the rounds of numerous places, got in and
out of the car, I took off and put on my fur, one dance and
off we went, I seemed to recognise so many faces, once we
lost Momina and found her at the door of the next room
talking and laughing with the door-man. I had no idea there

was so much doing in Turin. Momina stopped treating me
with her absent manner, she laughed in Morelli's face, she
even proposed we make the rounds of the dives along Porta
Palazzo where you drink red wine and the streetwalkers have
their beat. 'This isn't Paris, you know,' Morelli said. 'Be
satisfied with these four fancies.' In a basement night-club in
Via Roma, near the little square with the two churches,
Morelli pretended to strike a bargain for cocaine with the
drummer in the orchestra, they were great friends, we drank
a cocktail which he offered us: the drummer began to tell us
about when he played at the Royal Palace. 'His Highness . . .
because he's still His Highness to me . . .' To get rid of him
I danced with Momina. Dancing with a woman gives me an
uncomfortable feeling, but I wanted to test a suspicion I had
and this is still the quickest way. Nobody paid any attention
to us; Momina danced, talking into my ear, held me so tight
it burned, rubbed against me, laughed and breathed in my
hair, but it didn't seem to me that she wanted anything else;
she didn't make the least gesture; she was only a little crazy
and drunk. Well and good. It would have been a mess I really
didn't fancy.

And finally we arrived at the entrance to Morelli's block of
flats. He saw us a bit unsteadily into the elevator and talked
and talked. As he was opening the door to the flat he said:
'All this chit-chat prolongs one's life . . . Thank God I'm not
old yet, if I were old I'd be after girls to keep me company
. . . You're not girls, you're real women . . . Vicious and
malicious – yes – but women . . . You know how to talk . . .
No, no, I'm not old . . .'

We entered laughing and I liked the flat immediately. It
was obvious that it was empty and very large. We went
directly into the living-room which had large armchairs and
was full of rugs and azaleas. The big window opening on the
boulevard must have been nice in summer.

Brandy goblets in hand we made plans. Momina asked if I
was going to the mountains. There was still snow. Morelli

obstinately talked about Capri and the pine woods of Fregene, he tried to recall whether he had any business in Rome which would excuse a vacation or any sort of trip. I said it was strange that men should keep up appearances so. 'If it weren't for the men,' I said, 'we'd have had divorce in Italy long ago.'

'No need of it, really,' Momina observed tranquilly. 'You can always come to an understanding with your husband.'

'I admire Clelia,' Morelli said. 'She hasn't even wanted to try matrimony . . .'

'It's not that I want to butt into your private affairs,' Momina said looking at me, 'but if you got married would you like to have children?'

'Have you had them?' I laughed. 'That's what people get married for.'

But she didn't laugh. 'When you have children,' she said staring at her glass, 'you accept life. Do you accept life?'

'If you live you accept it, don't you?' I said. 'Children don't change things.'

'Yes but you haven't had any . . .' she said raising her eyes from her glass and looking at me.

'Children make a lot of trouble,' Morelli said, 'but women are all for them.'

'Not us,' Momina shot out.

'I've always noticed that a person who doesn't have children somehow is always imposed upon by people who want someone to mind *theirs*.'

'That's neither here nor there,' Momina interrupted. 'The point is that when a woman has a child she's no longer herself. She has to accept so many things, she has to say yes. And is it worth the trouble to say yes?'

'Clelia doesn't want to say yes,' Morelli said.

Then I said that talking about such things was senseless because everybody likes a baby but you can't always do what you want. If you want to have a child you have one, but you should be careful first of all to provide him with a home and means, so that afterwards he won't curse his mother.

Momina, having lit a cigarette, looked at me searchingly with her eyes half-closed against the smoke. She asked me again if I accepted life. She said that to have a child you had to carry it inside you and become like a sow and bleed and die – you had to say yes to so many things. That was what she wanted to know. Whether I accepted life.

'Oh, drop it,' Morelli said. 'Neither of you is pregnant.'

We drank some more cognac. Morelli wanted us to hear some records; he said that his servant slept soundly. From the floor above came a reverberation of feet and a great uproar. 'They're celebrating the carnival too,' he said so seriously that I burst out laughing. But I had been much struck by that business of saying yes; Momina had taken off her shoes and curled up in the armchair, smoking, we talked a lot of foolishness, she examined me with her dissatisfied air, cat-like, listening; I talked but inside I really felt bad. I had never thought about things the way Momina had talked about them. I knew they were just words, 'we're here to enjoy ourselves,' but anyhow it was nevertheless true that not to have children meant that you were afraid of living. I thought of the girl in the hotel, in her blue tulle and said to myself: It will turn out that she was going to have a baby. I was also a bit drunk and sleepy, but Morelli, on the other hand, became more and more like a young man as the time passed, he walked about the room, amused us, talked of getting breakfast. When we went out – he wanted at any cost to come – they took me to the hotel in the car; and so we didn't say anything more about those things that time.

# TEN

One of those days – it was drizzling – I was returning before evening from the vicinity of the Consolata. I had been looking for an electrician and seeing the old stores, the huge doors in the alleys and reading the street names – delle Orfane, di Corte d'Appello, Tre Galline – and remembering them, all had an effect on me. Not even the cobbles of the streets had changed. I didn't have an umbrella and, under the narrow slits of sky above the alleys, I once again inhaled the old odour of the walls. Nobody knows, I said to myself, that you are the Clelia they used to know. I hadn't dared pause and put my nose up against the old panes.

But when I was ready to return, I let myself go. I was in Via Santa Chiara and recognised the corner, the grated windows, the smeared, steamed glass of the shopfront. I stepped firmly across the threshold to the sound of the old bell and passing my palm over my fur, I felt it wet. The shelves of boxes with buttons sewn on the ends, the little counter, the odour of drygoods were still the same in that close air.

A lamp with a green reflector still lighted the cash-register. At the last moment I hoped that the business had changed hands, but the strong, resentful face of the thin woman who got up behind the counter was Gisella's. I believe I changed colour, and I hoped that I too had aged like that. Gisella inspected me, suspiciously, with a half-smile of invitation on her thin mouth. She was grey, but combed, clean and brushed.

Then she asked me, with a tone that once would have made

both of us laugh, if I wanted to buy something. I replied by winking. She didn't catch on and began the same phrase again. I interrupted her by thrusting out my hand. 'You haven't forgotten . . . ?' I said.

After the first pleasure and surprise, which still wasn't sufficient to give her colour (she had come out from behind the counter and we both went to the door to see each other better) we chatted and laughed and she looked at my fur and stockings with an appraising eye, as if I were her daughter. I didn't tell her everything that had happened to me or why I was in Turin; I let her think what she liked; I indicated vaguely that I lived in Rome and had a job. When we were children, Gisella was brought up so strictly that she used to complain to me of not even being allowed to go to the movies, and I used to tell her to come all the same.

She had already asked me if I was married and on my impatiently shrugging my shoulders she sighed, I don't know whether for me or for herself. 'I'm a widow,' she said. 'Giulio is dead.' Giulio was the son of the owner of the drapers shop; she had adopted Gisella, who was an orphan, and even in my time you could see she wanted Gisella to be her daughter-in-law. Giulio was a consumptive boy, very very tall, who wore a cape instead of an overcoat or heavy sweater, and in the winter he always sunned himself on the steps of the cathedral. Gisella never used to talk about Giulio; she was the only one who didn't believe that the old lady kept her in the house to marry her to the sick boy, and she used to say that he wasn't sick. Gisella was quick and judicious – at home she was pointed out as an example to follow.

'And Carlotta?' I asked. 'What's she doing? Still dancing?'

But Gisella had gone on to talk about the shop and told me the usual story – that she was glad to see me and be able to pour herself out to me. Then I was struck by the envy in her voice when she told me Carlotta had got along – she had been a dancer in Germany during the war, after which no one had seen her again. She returned to the subject of the store, told me how she had been bled white by Giulio's death – she had been paying sanatorium expenses until three years ago –; she told me about the old lady's death and of the bad times before the war. Her daughters – she had two, Rosa and Lina: the one coughed and was anaemic, the other, the fifteen-year-old, no; both were going to school and gave a lot of trouble, living was expensive and the shop no longer made money as it once did.

'But you're well-off, you still have that flat . . .'

It was nothing, she told me, nobody paid rent any more; she had had to evict the previous tenants and now she was renting it to a group of girls as a studio. 'Pays better. We're squeezed in upstairs.' I raised my head, I recalled the two rooms above, the narrow staircase, the little kitchen. When the old lady was there it was a risk going up, she was always standing at the head of the stairs calling Gisella and telling her not to go out into the street. I was struck by the fact that Gisella now behaved like the old owner, sighed, half-shut her eyes; even the resentful smile which she threw at my fur and stockings had a tinge of that envy with which the old lady had regarded the rest of us.

She called her daughters. I would have preferred to leave. This was all my past, intolerable and yet so different, so dead. I had told myself many times in those years – and later, too, as I thought it over – that the aim of my life was really to be a success, to become somebody and one day return to those alleys where I had been a child and enjoy the warmth, the amazement, the admiration of those familiar faces, of those little people. And I had been a success and I had returned; and the faces, the little people, had all disappeared. Carlotta was gone, and Slim, Giulio, Pia, and the old ladies. Guido also was gone. Neither we nor those times mattered any more to the people who were left, like Gisella. Maurizio always says that you get what you want, but only after you have no more need for it.

Rosa wasn't there, she had gone to the neighbour's. But

Lina, the healthy one, ran down the stairs, jumped into the shop; she stopped, cautious and reserved, outside the cone of light. She was dressed in flannel, not badly, and was well-developed. Gisella talked about making me coffee and taking me upstairs; I said it would be better if we didn't leave the shop. In fact, just then the bell rang and a customer entered.

'Ah yes,' Gisella said when the door closed again, 'we were girls who worked hard then . . . Other times. Aunt knew how to run things . . .'

She looked at Lina with a faint smile of pleasure. It was clear that the mother had chosen to work her fingers to the bone so that her daughters would not dirty their hands. She didn't even let Lina make the coffee. She ran upstairs herself to put it on. I exchanged a couple of words with the daughter – she looked at me complacently – I asked about her sister. A woman entered, ringing the bell and Gisella shouted down the stairs: 'Coming.'

I had said very definitely that I was just passing through Turin and leaving the next day: I didn't want obligations. But Gisella did not insist; she turned the conversation to the old lady, she made me talk about her in front of the daughter: about how the old lady ran things and gave advice to other people's daughters. This sort of thing happens all the time. With the excuse of raising her, of giving her a house and a husband, the old lady had made Gisella into her own image – and now she, Gisella, was working on her daughters. I thought of my mother, if she had been like that and whether it is ever possible to live with someone and run him without leaving the mark on him. I had escaped from my mother in time. Or had I? Mother had always grumbled that a man, a husband, was a pretty poor thing, that men were not bad, just fools – and, as you see, I had pretty well accepted her preaching. Even my ambition, the desire to go it alone, to be self-sufficient, didn't that come from her?

Before I left, Lina began to chatter about a school

companion and found the opportunity to speak badly of her, to wonder where the family found the means to send her to school. I tried to remember myself at that age, what I would have said in a case like this. But I hadn't gone to school, I hadn't drunk coffee with my mother. I was sure that Lina would talk about me behind my back to her mother just as she had talked to me about her school friend.

# ELEVEN

Only the hours I spent at Via Po didn't seem wasted. Or those I spent running around to find this and that and meeting various people at the hotel. By Ash Wednesday the masons and whitewashers had finished: the most difficult work still remained, that of furnishing. I was on the point of taking a train and going down to Rome to discuss everything again; you couldn't make yourself understood on the telephone. They said: 'We leave it up to you. Do what you like.' And the next day they telegraphed me to wait for a letter. The architect who was designing the interiors came to dine with me at the hotel: he had just returned from Rome and had a portfolio full of sketches. But he was young and he wanted to draw out the job; to avoid compromising himself he kept saying that all my suggestions were right. Looking at them here, all the pretty ideas from Rome collapsed. You had to take into account the dim light under the portico and keep in mind the decor of the other shops in Piazza Castello and Via Po. I became convinced that Morelli was right: the location was impossible – it was a quarter such as you no longer find in Rome, or perhaps only find on the outskirts. People walked in Via Po only on Sundays.

This architect was red, stubborn and hairy, a boy; he was always talking about mountain villas; as a joke he sketched the plan of a little glass house for winter sunbathing. He told me that he lived like me, without any fixed address; but differently from me in that I could wear – even tomorrow – whatever I created whereas only those pigs who had money

– nearly always robbed – could live in his villas. I got him to talking about the painters in Turin, about Loris. He got excited, took fire; he said he preferred house-painters. 'A house-painter knows colour,' he said. 'If he studied, a house-painter could become a fresco painter or a mosaicist tomorrow. No one can understand decoration unless he begins by painting walls. As for these artists . . . Who the devil do they paint for? And what the devil do they paint? Cloth! . . . They have no walls to paint. Their stuff's no good to anyone. Would you make a dress to keep under glass and not to wear?'

I told him that they didn't make just pictures and statues but that they also talked about putting on a play. They talked a lot about it. I told him some of the names. 'Oh fine!' he interrupted sarcastically. 'Fine! Fine! What would you say if that crowd put on a fashion show and invited Clelia Oitana to see it?'

Then we continued joking and came to the conclusion that only we window-dressers, architects and dressmakers were real artists. He ended, as I thought he would, by inviting me to go to the mountains to see an alpine hut he had done. I asked if he didn't have something a bit more comfortable to propose. Even a building in Turin. He looked at me with one eye closed, laughing.

'My studio . . .' he said.

I was sick of studios and talking. I almost preferred Becuccio and his leather wristband. The architect's name was Febo – I saw the signature at the bottom of all his projects. I laughed at him just as impertinently as he had at me and sent him to bed like a too clever boy.

But Febo was red, stubborn and hairy and he must have decided that I would do for him. He succeeded in discovering about Morelli and his cognac, about my visit to Loris's studio, and exactly how I stood with Mariella, Nènè and Momina. The next day he came and told me he wanted to take me to an art show. I asked if it wasn't better to decide on those curtains. He replied that the show was the best place, you had a liqueur and studied the furnishings of the place: it was enjoyable. We went, and we were just going up the steps when I heard Nènè laughing.

The rooms were a mixture of rough mountain furnishings and a twentieth century bar. Girls in checked aprons served us. Since the chairs and the crockery were also a part of the show, one was a bit uneasy, one felt exhibited in a show-window. Febo didn't say whether he had a hand in it too. Paintings and sculptures were up against the walls; I didn't look at them. I watched Nènè who, in her usual shabby suit laughed and laughed, crossing and uncrossing her legs and showing a good deal of them, while a waiter dressed in black leaned forward from behind and lit her cigarette. Momina was there, and other women and girls. A little old man with a Chinese beard had seated himself in front of Nènè and was sketching her portrait. A few people stood at the door and peeped in – the public getting a look at artists.

But Nènè soon became aware of me and came over and asked if I had seen her things yet. She was happy, excited, blew smoke into my face. Really, the large lips and the bangs made her a child. She led me to her statues – little deformed nudes that seemed mud. I looked at them, bending my head to one side; I thought – but did not say – that those were just the sort of children that would come out of Nènè's belly. She watched me avidly, open-mouthed, almost as if I were a handsome young man; I was waiting for someone to say something, I bent my head to one side. Febo came up from behind and catching both of us by the waist said: 'We're in the presence either of heaven or of hell. And it takes a little girl like you, Nènè, to reveal such terrors . . .'

A discussion sprang up in which Momina also took part. I paid no attention. I'm used to painters. I was watching Nènè's face, she followed the conversation wrinkling her forehead or being surprised at their words, as if everything depended on them. Had she really lost her boldness or was she just playing a part? Febo was the most incredible of all. Only the other day he had spoken so badly of Nènè and her things.

They talked about her good-humouredly and she played the part of the bewildered child to perfection. Her insisting on showing me her things had annoyed me. Couldn't she have let me see them by myself? But Nènè took care to keep up her reputation as a mannerless and impulsive girl. Perhaps she was right. Mariella's the only one absent, I thought. What would Becuccio say about these crazy people?

When I thought of Becuccio I burst out laughing. Febo turned to me suddenly, very jaunty, came up and putting his lips near my cheek whispered: 'You're a darling, Clelia. I bet you make better children.'

'Then you weren't serious about being in the presence of heaven or hell?' I replied. 'Nènè is still the sincerest person here . . .'

'This visceral art's given me an appetite,' he whispered. 'Let's go have a bit of sausage.'

Drinking *grappa* and eating sausage, he returned to the subject of the mountains. Even the old painter with the goatee was a competent climber. They were arranging an outing to the hut and assigning the duties; they had to telephone all over the place before tomorrow.

'You people go,' Momina said. 'I'm not going to the hut. Clelia and I will stop on the way . . .' And to me: 'Have you ever been at Montalto?'

# TWELVE

The Topolino stopped at a villa at the foot of the mountains. The two of us were alone. The other cars continued, they would wait for us at Saint Vincent. The few days of good weather had been enough to bring out the bloom of the greenhouse flowers, but the trees in the garden were still bare. I hardly had time to look around when Momina cried: 'Here we are.'

Rosetta was not wearing the blue dress this time. She came to meet us in a skirt and tennis shoes, her hair bound with a ribbon, as if we were at the seaside. She gave me a firm hand, gave the other to Momina, but did not smile: she had grey, searching eyes.

Her mother came out also, in slippers, fat and asthmatic, wearing a velvet dress. 'Rosetta can come back now,' Momina cried. 'The dances are all over in Turin . . .'

She gave her the latest news about friends, about the outing and the members of the party. I was surprised that Rosetta should accept her joking tone and should speak, like her, so self-possessedly; I asked myself if I really had seen her on that stretcher – how many days ago? Fifteen? Twenty? But perhaps Momina chattered on that way to help her, to relieve her and us of any embarrassment. They must have been very close friends.

It was her mother – poor thing – who had tearful, frightened eyes, who was upset in front of Momina and who looked at me with apprehension. She was so much the little lady that she bemoaned living in the country, the hardship of staying in the villa out of season. But Rosetta and Momina didn't encourage her. It ended with Momina's laughing at her. 'What an awful father,' she exclaimed, 'imprisoning the pair of you like this. You've got to escape, Rosetta. Agreed?'

'Agreed,' Rosetta said quietly.

Her mother was afraid it wasn't a good idea. 'You don't have skis, you don't have anything,' she said. 'Father doesn't know . . .'

'Who's talking about skiing?' Momina said. 'The others are crazy; let 'em go. We're going to Saint Vincent. Clelia hasn't come to ski . . .'

But first her mother wanted to give us tea, prepare the thermos, equip us. Rosetta had already run off to get dressed without wasting time.

We remained on the steps with her mother; Momina murmured: 'How is she?'

She turned around, with her hand on her cheek. I seemed to see her again, befurred, running in that corridor. She babbled: 'For heaven's sake. I hope nothing happens . . .'

'You've got to come back to town,' Momina cut in. 'You shouldn't hide yourselves away like this. Her friends in Turin are saying nasty things . . .'

We arrived at Saint Vincent, driving fast all the way through the mountains. Here too there was sun on the snow and not very many plants. I was surprised at the number of cars in the parking lot of the Casino.

'You've never been here?' Rosetta leaned forward to ask me. She had wanted to sit in the back, and during the drive she didn't look out of the window but perched forward in her fur jacket and talked to Momina.

'This is pretty convenient,' I said. 'Three hours by car.'

'Do you gamble?'

'I don't believe in luck.'

'There's nothing else in life,' Momina said, slowing down. 'People dream about having a car to come here to win enough for a car so that they can come back . . . That's the way the world is.'

She spoke with what seemed to me a definitely mocking tone. But neither of them laughed. We got out.

Luckily our friends had been scattered throughout the rooms for some time and we three could sit alone at the bar. It was jammed and like a hothouse. Rosetta had an orangeade and she sipped it quietly, looking at us. Her grey sunken eyes laughed very little. She seemed a quiet, outdoor girl, in her yellow sweater and knee-length trousers. She asked who was with us besides Pegi and the girls.

The conversation turned to her friends, to the latest doings in Turin. Momina said at one point that the play was being scuttled (she was smoking, and half-shut her eyes in the smoke).

'Why?' Rosetta asked coldly.

'They're afraid of making a reflection on you, . . .' Momina said. 'You know, the play ends unhappily . . .'

'Ridiculous,' Rosetta cut in. 'What does that matter?'

'You know who's still in favour of giving it?' the other said. 'Mariella. Mariella wants to give it and doesn't see any allusion in it. She says it doesn't matter to you . . .'

Rosetta glanced at me quickly. Getting up I said: 'Excuse me. I'm looking for the powder-room.'

They both looked at me, Momina with an expression of amusement.

I had a feeling that I had said something you don't say. While I walked through the corridors I kept repeating to myself, so I would calm down: You stupid fool. So this is how you're learning to be someone else. I believe I was still red.

I stopped in front of a mirror and caught a glimpse of Febo who came out of a gambling room. I didn't turn round until he had gone back in.

When I returned I said: 'Excuse me.'

And Rosetta, with those calm eyes of hers, said: 'But you

can stay. You don't bother us. I'm not ashamed of what I've done.'

Momina said: 'You saw Rosetta that night. Tell us how it was. The waiters hadn't undressed her, I hope?'

Rosetta's mouth twitched, as if she were trying to laugh. She was red, too. She became aware of it and hardened her eyes, staring at me.

I said something, I don't know what – that her mother and a doctor were around.

'No, no. I mean how Rosetta was,' Momina said, not letting up. 'The effect it had on an outsider . . . You were an outsider then . . . Whether her face was ugly and distorted; whether she seemed like someone else. Like when we're dead. After all, that was what she wanted.'

They must have been very good friends to talk like that. Rosetta looked at me out of her deep eyes, attentive. I said I'd been there only an instant, but that her face was swollen, she had on a blue evening gown and wore no shoes. Of that I was certain. Everything was so in order and so little disturbed that I had glanced under the stretcher to see if blood was dripping. It seemed like an accident, just a common accident. After all, a person who has passed out is like a person sleeping.

Rosetta breathed heavily, did not try to smile. Momina said: 'What time did you take the sleeping pills?'

But Rosetta didn't answer. She shrugged her shoulders, looked around and then asked hesitatingly in a low voice: 'You really believed I had shot myself?'

'If you really wanted to do it,' Momina said, 'shooting yourself would have been better. It didn't come off right with you.'

Rosetta looked at me out of her deep eyes, intimidated – at that moment she seemed to be somebody else – and she whispered: 'Afterwards you feel worse than you did at first. That's what's frightening.'

# THIRTEEN

There was no more time to talk about it. The girls saw us and came over, and faces of common acquaintances, even some from my hotel, popped up. Now that they knew we were here, Febo, Nènè and that chap Pegi I had met at Mariella's shuttled between the gambling rooms, where they carelessly played and lost, and the bar, where they downed brandy after brandy. It ended with Nènè and Pegi half-drunk, squabbling so much that the old painter and Momina intervened because the rest of us were leaving.

'We're coming too,' Momina said.

Meanwhile I wandered through the rooms, but the people packed around the tables got on my nerves, and there were large pictures on the walls, landscapes and nude women, almost as much as to say that the aim of all the gamblers was to live well and keep nude women in furs. What makes you mad is that you have to admit that everything really does come down to this and the gamblers are right. They're all of them right, even those who live by it, even the impoverished old ladies whose avid eyes seem to cash in the other gamblers' winning chips. At least, everybody's equal, gambling – well-born or low-born, whores, pickpockets, asses or bright boys, they're all after the same thing.

The moment came when Nènè, desperate, threw herself on a chair and shouted: 'Take me away, take me away.' Then we went to the cars and loaded the others in. It was only then that Nènè noticed Rosetta and began calling her and wanted to kiss her. Rosetta, obliging, made her leave off and lit a cigarette for her through the window.

They left. Now it was our turn. But looking at one another, laughter came over us. 'Let's have dinner in Ivrea,' Momina said, relieved, 'and then go back to Montalto.'

We went back into the rooms for a last look. Momina said she wanted to try to win the expenses of the trip, now that the jinxes had gone. 'Stick beside me,' she said to Rosetta; 'you're loaded with good luck, like the rope off a hanged man's neck.' They sat down at a table, very very serious. I stayed to watch. In a couple of turns Momina had lost ten thousand lire. 'You try,' she said to Rosetta. Rosetta lost another five thousand. 'Let's go to the bar,' Momina said.

Here we are, I thought, now it begins. 'Listen,' I said as I was drinking my coffee, 'I'll take you to dinner, but leave off it.'

'Lend me a thousand,' Momina said.

'Let's go,' Rosetta said. 'It won't do any good.'

I gave her the thousand and we lost that too. While we were in the foyer getting into our furs and Momina was going on about how she had lost, who should show up but that ass Febo, looking very sly.

'And where are the beautiful ladies going?' he grinned.

He hadn't left. Everybody had forgotten him. He had been in the gaming room while we were playing. 'You see, there you are,' Momina said, 'it's all your fault. Go away, go away . . .'

However, all four of us went to the Topolino and squeezed in. It wasn't easy to get rid of him the more so since he joked bitingly about the common jinx and said: 'You owe me something. We'll spend the night together.'

Febo knew Ivrea well, and he took us to a place frequented by carters. 'Nice,' Momina said when we entered. We went on through to a sort of back room which had a red hot terracotta stove, and the host, an ugly man with hair in his ears and a large apron, came and helped us off with our things, very attentive. 'Be careful there,' Febo said.

I was watching Rosetta getting out of her leopard jacket. 'Put all your furs together and this chap's hair would still be more than a match for them,' Febo whispered.

'Our architect's not so bad either,' Momina said.

'I'm not the only one,' he replied. 'How about Loris's hair? . . . How come he wasn't along?'

Momina turned to Rosetta. 'You used to like Loris once. He was so amusing.'

'As far as I'm concerned,' Febo said, 'hair's a great thing. Suppose Loris was *merely* degenerate? What the devil would he do? He would have had to give up his trade long ago. But with all that hair of his he gets off scotfree . . .'

'That's not amusing,' Rosetta said quietly. 'It's not amusing and it's not kind. You used to be friends.'

'Let's get her drunk, let's get her drunk,' Febo shouted. 'Then Rosetta can tell us about when everybody was friends with everybody . . .'

We ate the way you eat in such places, and drank likewise. The host suggested mysterious old wines from those regions; he and Febo winked at one another; after each dish he asked us if it had been to our taste. Even Rosetta livened up and joked; there was no more talk about Loris. Instead we joked about the alpinists who at that moment were eating cold canned meat in the hut Febo had designed, and Febo said with his mouth full: 'At least they're in tasteful surroundings.'

'I wish Morelli was along,' Momina said. 'He likes this sort of thing.'

'Who's Morelli?' Rosetta asked.

'He's an old gentleman who's got his name linked with Clelia's,' Momina said gaily. 'But of course you know him . . .'

'Oh, in other words,' Febo shouted, 'the handsomest aren't here. Take what you've got.'

Closing time came and with many smiles the host put us out. One good thing: we left it to Febo to pay him, by promise.

I wanted to pay but Momina said: 'Nothing doing. He's already cost us too much.'

We took Rosetta to Montalto. Her mother was still up waiting for her. She met us tearfully and while Febo kept trying to pull me into the back seat Momina stood outside arguing and made her promise that they would return to Turin the next day. I said goodbye to Rosetta, who gave me her hand through the window and shot me a glance at once peevish and grateful. We left.

'Why,' Febo said, pushing his head forward between our shoulders, 'why didn't they invite us to sleep at the villa?'

'Too many women for only one man,' Momina said.

'Why be stingy?' he said. 'Let's stop in Ivrea at least. I know a hotel . . .'

I didn't expect it but Momina accepted. 'Tomorrow we're going back to Montalto anyhow,' she said to me. 'And if we'd gone to the hut we would have slept out, wouldn't we?'

When he was arranging for the rooms, Febo said: 'Shame they can't give us one for three.'

Momina said: 'They'll give one for me and Clelia.'

We had hardly taken off our furs and washed (Momina had coldcream and perfume in her bag) when the door opened and Febo entered with a tray of liqueurs.

'Service,' he said. 'On the house.'

'Put it down there,' Momina said. 'Good-night.'

We couldn't get rid of him. After a bit Momina sat down on the bed and I lay down on the other side and wrapped myself in the covers. Febo, seated beside Momina, talked away. They talked about women, night-clubs in Turin. They said everything – absolutely everything – with a familiarity that was strange in two people who hadn't even met the day before. Febo, with great bursts of laughter, had tumbled back on the bed several times and ended by remaining there. Momina stretched out beside him. I drowsed off a couple of times, resignedly, and every time I waked suddenly, I found them stretched out there confabulating. Then I became aware that they had gone under the blankets together. At a certain point, a sudden jerk of Febo, I aimed a kick at him which got tangled in the covers. Then I sat on the edge of the bed and lit a cigarette. Momina hurried to the bathroom; Febo, his hair mussed, handed me a glass from the almost empty bottle. He was on me like a devil and tore off the covers.

He beat into me a bit and it was all over. Momina hadn't yet returned and Febo got to his feet beside the bed with his hair up like a dog's and brushed it down with his hand. 'Now will you let us sleep?' I yelled.

When he had gone out, I took off my dress and wrapped myself in the covers. I drowsed off before Momina returned.

# FOURTEEN

The next morning I was already downstairs drinking my coffee when Momina came down. I had left her with her face hidden in her short hair and her back bare as I had first seen her the evening of the ball. She appeared before me well got up but her eyes were ringed. She seated herself smiling, put down her bag and said quietly: 'We're a couple of early birds.'

She had some coffee and looked at me. 'Shall we go?' she said, putting down the cup.

'Shouldn't we pay first?'

'It would be nice, but do you really think we should?' She squinted at me with an absent air. 'Be a pleasant surprise for him when he wakes up. Brat.'

So we left. She didn't say anything else. We got into the car at the garage and were immediately in the country.

'It's too early to go to the Molas. Let's have a breath of air. Do you know the Canavese?'

So we drove around the Canavese, which was all hidden in drifts of mist, and sped through two or three towns.

Driving carefully, she said all of a sudden: 'Rosetta's really nice, isn't she?'

'What's this story about Loris?'

'A year ago,' Momina said, 'when Rosetta was painting. She took lessons from him. Then she quit. Loris was in the house all the time . . . You know how Loris is.'

'Like the friend last night.' I said.

Momina smiled. 'Not exactly.'

'You don't mean he's . . . ?' I popped out and then stopped.

'What?' Momina exclaimed, looking at me closely. 'Oh that
. . . No. Old gossip. I'd know.'

'A difficult girl . . . Suppose something like last night had
happened to her.'

'But she went to the hotel alone,' Momina said. 'She told
me. She doesn't fake with me. Only Adele sees love at the
bottom of everything . . . Rosetta understands these things.'

'Well, what did she poison herself for?' I asked. 'At her
age?'

'Not for love, I'm certain,' Momina said, wrinkling her
forehead. 'She lives the same sort of life I did, that all girls
live . . . We know perfectly well what pricks are . . .'

She was silent a bit, driving carefully.

'I don't know,' I said, 'but they can cause a lot of trouble.
It would be better if there weren't any.'

'Maybe,' Momina chattered on. 'But I'd miss 'em. Wouldn't
you? Imagine all the men nice and dignified and respectable.
There'd never be any more flashes of truth. Nobody would
have to come out of his den any more and show himself as
he really is, ugly and piggish as he is. How could you really
know men?'

'I think you like to enjoy them.' I got that far and then
stopped. I realised that I was a fool. I realised that Momina
was worse than me and that she laughed at such things.

But she didn't laugh. She whistled a light disdainful whistle.
'Shall we go back?' she said.

The humming of the motor was making me drowsy and I
thought about the night, about Febo's red hair. The light mist
under the sun gave me a sense of freshness and suddenly
there came into my mind the tiled dairy shop which I had
entered alone so many mornings before hurrying off to the
shop, while Guido slept satiated in my bed.

'Well, what do you think Rosetta did it for?' Momina
suddenly asked.

'I don't know,' I said. 'Maybe –'

'It just doesn't make sense,' she cut in. 'She looks at you

with those frightened eyes . . . keeps closed up like a clam
. . . keeps it all inside herself. She never mentioned anything
to us. You know what I mean . . .'

When we arrived at Montalto the shutters were still closed
but a chilly sun filled the garden. Momina was telling me how
at times she herself was seized, not by the momentary nausea
you get from this or that person, or from an evening or a
season – but by an utter and complete disgust with living,
with everything and everyone, with time itself which goes so
fast and yet never seems to pass. She lit a cigarette and
sounded the horn.

'We'll talk about it another time,' she said laughing.

The gardener opened the gate. We rolled up on the gravel.
When we got out in front of the steps, the mother, frightened,
appeared at the door.

'There's so damned much that doesn't make sense,'
Momina added.

We set off for Turin like a caravan. Rosetta with us; her
mother with the maid and the chauffeur in the big car which
had come up specially from Turin. All morning, while waiting
for the big car, we had sauntered about the villa and the
garden talking and looking at the mountains. Once I was alone
with Rosetta; she had taken me upstairs to a terrace where,
as a child, she told me, she had stayed by herself hour after
hour to read and look at the tops of the trees. Down there –
she said – was Turin, and in the summer evenings on that
terrace she used to think about the seaside towns she had
been in, about Turin, about the winter, about the new faces
that she would some day meet.

'They often fool you,' I said, 'don't you think?'

She said: 'You just have to look into their eyes. Everything
is in their eyes.'

'There's another way of knowing them,' I replied. 'Working
with them. When people work they give themselves away.
It's difficult to fool someone about work.'

'What work?' she said.

So we sped towards Turin and I was thinking that neither she nor Momina knew what work is; they had never earned a meal or a pair of stockings or the various trips they had made or were making. I thought how funny it was that we all work so that we won't have to work and how you get mad when someone doesn't have to work. I thought of Rosetta's mother, whose work was to take care of her daughter, to run after her, to see she wasn't without anything; and how her daughter repaid her with those scares she gave her. I thought of Gisella and her daughters; the little shop, 'we're squeezed in upstairs,' and all to keep them from doing anything, to keep them on velvet. I became nasty. I saw Febo's face. I started to think of Via Po.

I went there before evening, first taking a bath at the hotel. Nobody had come to call on me, not even Morelli. But on the table there was a bouquet of lilacs with a telegram from Maurizio. 'This too,' I thought. Doing nothing all day I had time to think of these things. It was exactly a month since I had left Rome.

I found Becuccio supervising the arrival of the crystal chandeliers. He wasn't wearing the grey-green trousers or the heavy sweater any more, but a wind-breaker with a yellow scarf. He always wore the wrist-band. His curly hair and white teeth had a curious effect on me. While I was talking I was very nearly on the point of stretching out my hand and touching his ear. It's the mountain air, I thought frightened.

Instead I became very cold with him over the lateness of the shipments. 'The architect . . .' he said.

'The architect has nothing to do with it,' I cut in. 'It's your job to keep after the suppliers . . .'

Together we checked the crystals and I liked the way his large hands felt about in the straw for the brackets and pendants. In the newly plastered room, under the unshaded light bulb, the prisms shone like rain in the beam of headlights. We held them up against the light, he said: 'It's like when you're cutting tracks with an acetylene torch.' He had been a worker on the night shift for the tramline – the usual story. Suddenly I felt him take my hand in the straw. I told him to be careful.

'That stuff's expensive.'

'I know,' he replied.

'All right then,' I said. 'Let's get on with the boxes.'

# FIFTEEN

The people in Rome talked as though the shop could be got ready by mid-March, but the vaulting on the first floor still had to be done. Working with Febo became difficult; he began saying that they didn't understand anything in Rome and that if I didn't know how to get my way he did. He had returned from Ivrea with an air of pretending that nothing had happened; he didn't mention the hotel bill but he treated me more familiarly. I told him that I took orders in Rome but in Turin I gave them and how much did he want for having been troubled. Without raising my voice I let him have it good. The next day a bouquet arrived which I gave to Mariuccia.

But Rome was a constant headache. In a long evening phone call they gave me the news: the shop and the windows were to stay as originally designed, but the furnishings in the fitting-rooms and the large salon on the first floor were to be changed, to be named according to the style in which they would be decorated. It was necessary to find mirrors, stuffs, lamps, prints, but they didn't know yet whether it was to be baroque or what. I had to tell the architect, make plans, take photographs, send someone to Rome. Suspend everything. Rugs and curtains too.

'For the fifteenth?' I said.

They didn't care when. Better sooner of course. However, by the end of the month.

'Too little time,' I said.

'Send the architect here.'

I didn't send him, I went myself. The next evening I bathed

in my own apartment and, after airing the rooms, I was walking on the usual cobbles. Two infernal days of sirocco followed in which I saw the usual bored faces and no one ever got to the point. That was Rome, I knew. Halfway through a conference somebody or other would come in, his turn to talk would come up, he would get up and say: 'You've got to keep accounts.' Someone was always missing, the one who had called the conference. Madame was on the point of bringing down Febo too, but gave up the idea. We had our most orderly conference at a table in the Columbia while the others were dancing. All I succeeded in doing was to convince her it was best to open definitely in May with the summer styles, but I got an idea of what they had in mind. Somebody had said that Turin is such a difficult city. I explained that there are limits to what you can do in Turin, too.

Even Maurizio unexpectedly got bored. He thought it was his duty to wait for me, to stay beside me, to follow me. He avoided mentioning Turin. I didn't tell him about Morelli. I was aware that I was much more alone in Rome, climbing up those streets or entering Gigi's for coffee, than I had been in Turin in my hotel bed or in Via Po. The last evening we came in late under a wind that rocked the street lamps and rattled the shutters. I didn't tell him that certain half-words and silences of Madame made it clear that they were putting me in charge of the Turin shop and that I wouldn't be able to come back to Rome. I told him to stay in bed the next morning and not come to the station.

It was drizzling in Turin. Everything was chilly, melancholy and foggy; if I hadn't known it was March I would have thought it November. When Febo heard that I had come back from Rome, there he was with his cigarette between his lips and his mouth twisted round so that the smoke wouldn't get in his eyes; but he was not too sure of himself. When I told him about the baroque, he looked at me amused.

'And now, Clelia,' he said softly, 'what are you going to do?'

'Look for a decorator who knows something about baroque,' I said.

'Turin's full of baroque. It's all over the place, but never baroque enough . . .'

'They know that in Rome,' I said, 'but they don't know what baroque is.'

'Here. We can do it like this,' he said, and began throwing off sheet after sheet of rapid sketches.

He sketched and smoked all evening. He was clever, all right. I watched that red, bony hand fly over the paper, scarcely aware that it was his. It made me angry that despite his youth he knew so much, that he could play with his knowledge and talent the way he did; they had cost him no effort – like finding money in his pocket that he hadn't put there. He had told me before that he only went to architecture classes on days when he knew he would find a certain girl there. That he had learned his trade travelling around the world with his mother, a crazy old lady, who furnished, changed and refurnished houses, as though they were so many hats to trim. He explained lightly that it wasn't necessary to change the little salons at all, just to find the pieces at the antique dealers', and they didn't all have to be baroque – some could even be provincial pieces, of the worst possible taste – and to arrange them well, in the right place and give them stage lighting. He laughed about it and tried to kiss me. We were in the hotel drawing-room. I raised my hand and he kissed that.

The next day Morelli came, excited, asking me where I had been the past few days. I told him that he had to help me because the young people of Turin were really too flighty and we old people had to maintain a united front. I asked him if he knew the antique dealers and the museum.

When he understood what I wanted he asked me if I was setting up house in Turin.

Then we went to Via Po and I showed him the rooms.

'What do your painter friends say?' he asked me.

'If only they understood something about paintings . . .'

'In here the only paintings you'll want will be mirrors,' he said seriously, indicating the bare walls. 'You don't want to make your customers disappear. There's no painting so good as a beautiful woman undressing.'

He accompanied me to the antique dealers along Via Mazzini and meanwhile we talked about Rome. 'It would be easier in Rome,' I said. 'Rome is full of old mansions being liquidated . . .'

Well, I found out that they didn't fool around in Turin either. Those shops were the honey and we the flies. You could hardly move among the mountains of stuff – ivory pieces, peeling canvases, grandfather clocks, figurines, artificial flowers, necklaces, fans. At first glance everything seemed like old junk, but after a bit you saw there wasn't a piece – not a miniature or an umbrella handle – that you didn't want to have around you or put in a house. Morelli said: 'They aren't showing us the best. They don't know who we are,' and he looked at me judiciously and said: 'My wife should be along.'

Crossing the street he said: 'What do you think about all this stuff?'

I said: 'It hurts me to think that when you die your stuff ends up like this in other people's hands.'

'It's worse when it ends up like that before you're dead,' Morelli remarked. 'If our beautiful friend were here she would say that we too pass from hand to hand of those who desire us . . . The only thing that saves people is money . . . which passes into everyone's hands.'

Then the talk shifted to women and houses and Donna Clementina, who was a girl when some of those parasols and guitars and mottled mirrors were new. 'She knew how to set herself up. No man can say he had her in hand . . . I have to laugh when I think of Mariella's friends – these boys and girls who have all the vices without any experience . . . They think all you have to do is talk. I'd like to see them in twenty years . . . The old lady got where she wanted to go . . .'

We entered another shop. We didn't talk about baroque. I told Morelli that it was better to see a palace, a house, to get a more natural idea of the stuff. 'Let's go to Donna Clementina's,' he said. 'That evening there were too many people, but the porcelains alone are worth . . .'

# SIXTEEN

We arrived just as some women were leaving; they stared at me. Twenty years ago my route never went through that quarter of Turin. We visited with Mariella and her mother who had just had tea; the grandmother – unfortunately – was napping; she was preparing for the evening when a Romanian violinist would come to play and she wanted to be present. A few friends were expected, would we care to join them?

Mariella looked at me reproachfully and while we were going into the room with the porcelains she scolded me for not having told her in time about the trip to Saint Vincent. 'Come this evening,' she said. 'Rosetta and the whole crowd will be here.'

'I haven't seen anybody for ages. What are you up to now?'

'I can't tell,' she said, mysteriously. 'You'll have to see to find out.'

I pulled Morelli's coat-tail just in time to keep him from telling those gossips the story of my fitting-rooms. Mariella's mother lit the showcase lights and told us something about each piece. She spoke of her great grandfather, of weddings, of aunts, of the French Revolution. Morelli told us the names of some of the pink, bewigged women in the miniatures hanging on the walls. He recounted the story of a certain Giudetta – another member of the family – who had lain down under a tree in the royal gardens and the king of that epoch let cherries fall through the branches into her mouth. I looked closely and tried to understand the things themselves, what they were made of and the secret touch or trick that made them them – as you do with gowns – it was more than difficult, it was useless. The elegance of the figurines and the little painted portraits of the miniatures was made of nothing, and without the names, the conversation and the family stories they couldn't create an atmosphere in a shop. I really had to rely on Febo.

So that evening we returned to listen to the violinist. I saw the fierce old lady again, with her shawl and her ribbon round her neck, again I saw the circle of men with wrinkled foreheads, the lamps, the rug. There were fewer young people than the other time, they sat suffering on the up-holstered chairs, Loris wasn't among them. Rosetta and Momina smiled at me.

The violinist played well, as they do on such occasions. He was a fat little man with white hair, who kissed the hands of all the women; it wasn't clear whether he was paid or had come as a friend. He laughed with his tongue in his cheek and looked at our legs. A lymphatic lady wearing glasses and a rose at her shoulder accompanied him on the piano. The women exclaimed: 'Bravo!' All in all, I was bored.

Morelli clapped, enthusiastic. When tea came I looked for Rosetta and Momina. 'As soon as the old lady gets up,' we said, 'we'll go too.'

Mariella cornered me: 'I'm coming too,' she said. 'Wait for me.'

She ended by dragging along everyone, including the violin-ist. Outside the large entrance door the bespectacled lady started to shout: 'The maestro wants to treat us.' Everybody was speaking French.

In the car I found myself next to Rosetta. I said in the dark and confusion: 'It's turned out badly. Ivrea was better.'

'It's not morning yet,' Momina said, getting in. For the violinist, who was with the women and Morelli in Mariella's big car, treating us meant circling around the centre of town, stopping in front of the cafés, putting his head out, arguing and then giving a signal to start off again. After three or four of these tricks, Momina said: 'Oh, go to the devil' and started off on her own.

'Where are we going?'

'To your hotel,' she said.

We entered the salon gaily and noisily. Several people raised their heads.

'Doesn't it give you the shivers?' she said to Rosetta, who walked between us with clenched fists.

Rosetta smiled thinly. She said: 'There's a possibility nobody paid my bill. Hope they don't throw us out . . .'

'You never came back?' Momina asked.

Rosetta shrugged her shoulders.

'Where shall we sit?' I asked.

The waiter brought us three cognacs. Behind the bar Luis winked at me.

'Let's hope Mariella doesn't find us,' I said. 'I'm afraid the Romanian won't treat much.'

'There are a lot of 'em,' Rosetta said. 'Somebody will pick up the bill . . .'

Then I said it was funny but in Turin I had to avoid people. There were so many painters, so many vain, inflated nobodies, so many musicians – a new one everywhere you turned, not even in Rome were people so continuously on holiday. And there was Mariella, too, who wanted to act at all costs. You'd have thought there'd never been a war . . .

Rosetta, twirling her brandy glass, smiled from the chair. 'You're talking about us too,' she said in a low voice. 'Why do we lead such lives?'

'I don't know,' I said. 'It seems to me that so much to-do isn't worth the effort.'

Momina who hadn't yet sat down paced restlessly between us and the bar. 'Nothing's worth the effort,' she said. 'Before the war you could travel at least.'

Then she threw herself into a chair and put her hand down to take off her shoes. 'I'm afraid it's not done here,' she said. 'Haven't you got a couple of comfortable chairs in your room?'

We went up in the lift. I watched Rosetta's movements. We came out into the corridor and she looked at me quickly; I made a gesture to indicate that it had happened here.

'All these corridors are alike,' she said, staring at Momina's back.

'Like the days of the year,' Momina said. 'All the doors are alike, and the beds and the windows and the people who sleep here for one night . . . You've got to have Clelia's courage to live here . . .'

'Or hers,' I said, indicating Rosetta.

'Listen,' Momina said, without turning around, 'now that they're bringing up our cognac, if you like we'll put out the lights and you can tell us how you ended up here and mistook the dosage . . . I still don't believe . . .'

Suddenly Rosetta stopped, very pale, clenched her fists and bit her lips. But we were at the door and I said: 'Let's go in.' Rosetta entered without saying anything. No one spoke between the time we sat down (Momina throwing her shoes off to one side) and the waiter put the tray on the table, and I became aware that Rosetta's eyes were filling with tears. Momina hadn't noticed anything.

'Aren't you going to sit down, Rosetta?' she said.

Rosetta shook her head angrily, went to the door, turned out the lights and replied in a hoarse voice: 'There.'

For several moments only the red tip of Momina's cigarette showed in the dark. You heard the distant rattling of a tram. I made out the lighter rectangle of the window.

'Are you mad at me?' Momina said mockingly.

I could feel Rosetta's effort to control her voice. She didn't succeed. She stammered slowly: 'You . . . you shouldn't . . . laugh . . .'

'I do it to buck you up,' the other said coldly. 'I do it for your own good. Try to be intelligent. You are, you know. What's happened? I've done nothing. Have I insulted you? Have I told you to do this or not do that? I've only helped you see clearly when you've got into your messes . . . Does that scare you? I understand one's wanting to kill oneself . . . everybody thinks of it some time or other . . . but one's got to do it right, do it so that it's real . . . Do it without recriminations . . . Instead you act like an abandoned dressmaker's assistant . . .'

'I . . . hate you,' Rosetta babbled, breathing heavily.

'But why?' Momina said, serious. 'What have you got to reproach me for? For having been too much to you, or too little? What does it matter, we're friends.'

Rosetta didn't reply and Momina didn't continue. I heard her breathe. I put down my glass blindly. I murmured: 'Sit down.'

She sat down. I realised that I could talk. Then I said that though it was no affair of mine, seeing that we were together I had a right to say a word too. I had heard all kinds of stories about what she had done and none was true. 'If it's a matter between the two of you,' I said, 'say what you have to say and get it over with.'

Momina twisted around in the armchair, looking for a cigarette. The light of her match nearly blinded me, I caught a glimpse of the two of them through my eyelashes.

'What is it? Have you made love together?'

Neither replied. Momina began to laugh and cough.

# SEVENTEEN

'You can't even say that's it,' Momina started off again, querulously; by that time I could finally make out their faces again in the dark. 'It's a good thing you put out the lights, dear. Can't you convince yourself that you've made a personal matter, an hysterical drama, out of something that could have been beautiful and had some sense? . . . Did you hear what Clelia said?'

She had heard, and she must have been burning red. I don't think she was crying any more or was afraid. 'You two have nothing to do with it,' she said nastily, in her unreasonable voice. 'I'm twenty-three, I know what life is. I don't have it in for anyone. Let's talk about something else if you don't mind.'

'At least tell us what it feels like. Whom one thinks about at that moment. Did you look in the mirror?'

She didn't talk teasingly but with a child's voice as if she were acting. Before, when the lights went out, it had seemed to me a scene on the stage. Again the notion came to me that there had been absolutely no one on the stretcher that evening.

Rosetta said she hadn't looked in the mirror. She didn't remember if there were any mirrors in the room. She had turned out the lights then, too. She didn't want to see anything or anybody, only to sleep. She had a tremendous, a terrible headache. Which suddenly went away, leaving her stretched out and happy. How happy she was. It seemed a miracle. Then she woke up, in the hospital, under a lamp which hurt her eyes.

'Disgusted?' Momina murmured.

'Uh,' Rosetta said. 'Waking up is horrible . . .'

'I knew a cashier in Rome,' I said, 'who went crazy from seeing herself all the time in the mirror behind the bar . . . She got to thinking she was somebody else.'

Momina said: 'One should look at oneself in the mirror . . . You've never had the courage, Rosetta . . .'

We talked on like that, about mirrors and the eyes of a person killing himself. When the waiter came with another tray, we lit the lights. Rosetta's face was calm and hard.

The telephone rang. It was Mariella and she wanted to know what had happened. She couldn't make out what I said because an orchestra was blaring away at her end. I looked questioningly at the other two. I shouted into the telephone that I had come home because I was tired. That they should dance and have a good time. That it had been a pleasant evening.

Then Rosetta used the telephone. She called her house. She said: 'Mama, I'm coming back now.' Momina put on her shoes and they went away.

The next day Rosetta paid me a visit in Via Po. She entered with an uncertain smile, in her leopard jacket. Febo was upstairs with Becuccio taking certain measurements. 'You don't want to meet our friend,' I said. 'Do you want to go shopping with me?' She waited for me in the large room while I shouted up the stairs that I was going out. Seeing her so young standing there beside the window, I thought: Exchange her for Mariella and you'd have a perfect cashier there.

As we were walking along under the porticoes, I told her that I had thought of giving her a job. She smiled in that soft way of hers. 'I've got an idea,' I said. 'A shop staffed by your most distinguished friends. Would you be in on it? The best names in Turin . . . One at the cash register, one behind the showcases, others in the fitting-rooms . . .'

She took up the joke. She said: 'Who'd come to buy? There'd be nobody left.'

'Your servants, I suppose . . . People without names.'

'We wouldn't know how to do anything . . .'

'Who knows . . . Like charity picnics and dances . . .'

'I envy you, Oitana,' she said. 'It's nice to work as you do.'

'Sometimes it's hell . . . There's always a boss.'

'Maybe that's what work is. Having someone to tell you what to do or not to do . . . It's a salvation.'

'Try telling your maid that.'

She hesitated. 'Yesterday,' she said, 'I was a fool . . .'

I didn't interrupt her, and she went on: '. . . One says and does lots of false things . . . You understand. I'd like to be someone else, like that cashier in Rome . . . Even crazy like her. You mustn't believe what Momina says . . . At times Momina's exasperating . . .'

'She's been more discreet than me . . .' I said, hesitatingly, holding her eye.

'You know a lot about life, Oitana . . .' She searched for words. 'You wouldn't think much of two women who talked the way we did yesterday, would you . . . ?'

She had stopped, stubborn, and was devouring me with her eyes. Yesterday evening, in the dark, she must have been just as red.

I made her move on. I told her that as long as a woman can blush you can't say anything about not thinking much of her. She excused herself. She said: 'I always blush over nothing.' I told her that everything you do is all right so long as you don't damage your health and don't get bad ideas into your head. I asked her if that was the reason she had taken the veronal.

We had stopped in front of the florist's in Via Pietro Micca. It was easier to talk. I said: 'Shall we send some flowers to Mariella for yesterday?'

'Let's,' she said.

We chose lilies of the valley. While the woman arranged the green, I said to Rosetta: 'At your age they aren't vices, vices come later.'

'I don't think I have any,' she said wryly. 'It would be better if I did.'

When we had returned under the porticoes I asked her what game we were playing at now. She hadn't tried to kill herself for that?

Rosetta, surprised, told me that she had no idea herself why she had gone to the hotel that morning. In fact, when she entered, she was happy. She was feeling relieved after the dance. For a long time nights made her shudder, the idea of having got through another day, of being alone with all her disgusts, of waiting for morning stretched out in bed – all became unbearable. That particular night, anyhow, she had already got through. But then precisely because she hadn't slept but paced back and forth in the room thinking of night, thinking of all the stupid things that had happened to her in the night and now she was again alone and couldn't do anything, little by little she became desperate and finding the veronal in her bag . . .

'Wasn't Momina at the dance?'

No, Momina wasn't, but at the hotel she, Rosetta, stretched out in bed, had thought a lot about her, had thought about many things Momina had said, their conversations, Momina's courage – Momina who was even more disgusted with life but who laughed and said: 'I'll wait till the weather's better before killing myself, I don't want to be buried in the rain.'

Rosetta said: 'But I didn't have the patience to wait any longer . . .'

'You and Momina haven't fought?'

'No, we argue sometimes, like last night, but we're good friends. Momina's the only friend I have.'

How much that meant I didn't know. I said sharply: 'Only a friend?'

She looked at me, thin, with her cat eyes. She began to blush faintly, and then she controlled herself nervously.

'What are you trying to make me say, Oitana?' she brought

out jerkily. 'Is it necessary? But I'm not ashamed. You know how it is among girls. Momina was my first love. A long time ago, before she got married . . . Now we're just friends, believe me . . .'

# EIGHTEEN

I had to believe her. I asked her why she didn't think of getting married. She shrugged her shoulders. She said she knew what men are. 'Perhaps not all,' I observed.

'It's not necessary,' she said.

'Don't tell me that you're like Momina – afraid of having babies.'

'I like babies,' she said. 'But they ought to stay babies. When I think that afterwards they grow up and become persons like us, I get mad . . . Don't you feel that way too?'

'I don't have any,' I said.

We left promising to meet again, but I was sure that she wouldn't come back. Rosetta had come to see me either because she was ingenuous or because she didn't think much of me, but now she must have realised that it was impossible to re-establish the initial distance between us. We always came back to the same subject.

I went to Milan to inspect some glass tables and shelves with Febo who borrowed a car for the trip. Everything went well, except that on the way back when we stopped to light our cigarettes, Febo, with the look in his eyes that he had that night in Ivrea let his hands start wandering. I gave him such a black eye that I thought I had blinded him, but starting off again he behaved and I told him that the world was large and that you shouldn't make love with your colleagues. He watched the road sheepishly. I asked why he didn't try again with Momina, or even find himself a wife among Momina's

friends. Rich and educated people who knew how to paint and
put on plays. Then he looked at me, amused, out of his one
good eye. He stopped the car. Oh, oh, here we are again, I
thought. 'Clelia, Clelia,' he said without touching me, 'do you
want to be my wife this evening?'

'Is that a serious proposal?'

'We're already husband and wife. You beat me.'

'I could be your mother.'

'Yes, yes,' he said and clapped his hands. 'Yes, mam. Can
I go in the woods and collect snails?'

However, we stopped to dance at a pavilion in a town
outside Turin and Febo, good-humouredly, began to quarrel
with a young couple dancing who blocked our way. They
threatened to give him another black eye. It was astonishing
how Febo, blond and hairy, took chances in that country place
where he didn't even know the dialect. I told him to cut it out
and I had to pull him away. Then he suggested dinner in some
dive, and he asked if I didn't like to break out of the everyday
round and do crazy things like that.

'That's not difficult,' I said. 'What's unpleasant is having a
dive as the centre of your everyday round.'

'Well, let's do something unpleasant,' he said.

We found a little joint where Corso Giulio Cesare starts on
the outskirts of Turin. At first Febo behaved properly and
we thought about eating. But the host wasn't like the hairy
chap in Ivrea and their kitchen wasn't much. A red-eyed girl
in slippers brought us the dishes and she looked at my
stockings; and the other people there, an old lady and some
truck drivers, watched us. The room was cold, newly painted
and already dirty; I thought of how back in my time this was
all countryside, open roads and countryside. 'The things we
do really are unpleasant,' I said to Febo.

He tried to liven up and find the wine good. Behind the bar
the girl watched us with her red eyes. The others were now
playing cards, smoking and spitting.

When we had finished the omelette, I suggested we go.

'But there must be a place around here . . .' he said. When we went out it was dark. A wind blew against the red neon signs along the avenue. 'This city is beautiful in its own way,' Febo said. 'You don't understand, you live too much among the gentry.'

I got into the car mad enough to throttle him. 'It's you people, those stupid girls, the Martellis and the Mominas who like to act like gentry,' I said. 'I was born in Turin. I know what it's like to see someone else wearing silk stockings and not to have them yourself . . .'

While we argued and he was cackling derisively, we stopped again, in front of a café with an illuminated garden.

'Blood flows here nights,' he said.

The light came from the windows of a large room lit by naked bulbs. There wasn't any orchestra, a radio played and several couples danced on the cement ring and shrieked. I knew what those places were like.

'If you don't like the common room,' Febo said in my ear, 'there's a room upstairs . . .'

I said I'd have a cup of coffee but I didn't want to stay long. We weren't proper company for one another in such a place. 'There's the possibility that I'd drop you,' I said, 'and go with that character wearing the foulard.'

Febo looked at the boy with the foulard who was chattering at a table with two women with mussed lipstick. He raised an eyebrow. He didn't answer and leaned his back against the bar.

'That boy,' I said, 'doesn't dream of coming to our places to spend the evening. As long as he lives the way he lives he doesn't feel that he has to go to some elegant place. For him red and green ties and the perfumes you buy at cigarette counters are elegant. He works with those girls . . . Why amuse yourself at his expense?'

Febo planted his elbows on the bar behind him and looked at the fellow. Not being drunk yet, he grumbled: 'Who's talking now? . . . The woman or the colleague?'

I called him a fool and said I was serious.

And then he looked at me and asked what sort of place I was born in.

'Like this, more or less,' I said dryly.

The young man with the foulard had become aware that Febo was staring at him and now he looked at us. 'And you,' Febo said, looking disdainfully about the room, 'you got out of your environment, put on silk stockings and now you amuse yourself at the expense of us respectable and educated people. Who asked you to?'

While speaking he had stared at the foulard who had moved and come up to him. I felt something brewing in the room and I was blinded by anger, fear and an instinct for stopping the foulard. I slapped Febo in the face with all my might, yelled something and dragged him off by the arm. Everybody laughed and gave way. We got to the car under a shower of laughter and insults hurled from the door.

I said: 'Get going, you fool.'

He started up with clenched teeth and crossed over the Dora as if the bridge was collapsing behind us. 'I want to get out here,' I said.

His face was half-resentful, half-laughing. 'And I want to drink,' he shouted. 'They treat me like a drunk. I might at least be one.'

My hands were still shaking and I kept quiet. I let him run on. But I seemed to have taken that slap myself, and I couldn't calm down. I said to myself: 'He's no worse than the others. In his circle they're all like that.' I kept saying it over and over to myself and wondered if it was worth the effort to work and get where I had got and then find I was no longer me and even worse than Momina who at least lived among her own kind. Other times when I thought these things I always consoled myself by saying that it wasn't the things I had obtained or the place I had carved out for myself but the act of carving it out and obtaining them that made my life worthwhile. This, too, is a destiny, I said to myself, and nobody made it but me. But my hands were shaking and I couldn't calm down.

Finally I said drily that I wanted to get out. I opened the door. Then Febo began kissing me wherever he could put his lips, moaning; then he stopped. I jumped out and went off.

# NINETEEN

It's not easy to avoid leisured people. When I returned to the hotel I found an invitation to a de luxe auction, with a note initialed by Morelli saying he would phone me the next day. It began to sink in on me that if I had rented a room on arriving in Turin I would never have met Morelli or anyone. Except Febo, unfortunately. But that was the kind of life I was living – useless to lament the loss of the calm disorder of my life in Rome. These things pass away by themselves. Many times in past years I had found myself in a similar whirl. It was almost laughable: of all that only Maurizio was left. And how long would he be left?

For several days the work in Via Po discouraged me. They wanted me there all the time. I had to run around, to think of everything, to hunt about in every corner of Turin. Twenty years ago I wouldn't have dreamt it possible. Since when had I been so clever? It was as though I too was putting on a play like the leisured people of Turin, and after all it was only right that I should always find them under foot if I was working for them. When these ideas occur to me I'd like to be able to get away, to drop everything, to return to the workshop.

Even Becuccio had his say on the matter of the antique furniture. He knew of a couple of cabinet-makers, father and son, who worked at the Royal Palace before the war and had done some delicate restorations. We went to look for them. They were at the back of a courtyard up a dirty, narrow alley, but inside it was an old palace, there were even some trees and a statue. The cabinet-maker, a little old man who touched his glasses suspiciously, began to chatter in the open courtyard. When he understood what we wanted, he told me it was a shame to put beautiful furniture in a shop. Modern stuff, veneered and enamelled, would do. I told him that we'd already gone over that, but that I wanted to see something. What did I want to see, he said, since the palaces were all closed? I didn't want to see the palaces, I said, all I wanted was an idea, to get oriented. He said that if I didn't want to see, it was clear that I didn't understand anything about it and in that case I might as well put the usual stuff in the shop.

Becuccio asked him if he didn't have some work under way. The old man turned to the open shop and shouted into the dark. Somebody in the rear moved. 'Do we have anything?' the old man shouted. The other grunted. 'There isn't anything,' said the old man, touching his glasses. 'What do you expect, you don't have the heart to work for people any more.'

Becuccio was irritated and began to lecture him, and I had to drag him away too. The cabinet-maker had retreated into his shop and didn't even reply. We returned together to Via Po, where Febo was waiting for me to select the stuffs to put on the walls. I told Becuccio that it was pleasant to live like that old man: slam the door in people's faces and work only on what you liked.

'He can't have much work,' Becuccio said. 'Politics has gone to his head . . .'

Then I went to the auction with Morelli, and there were some really beautiful grandfather clocks and sets of tableware. Every now and then a 'This would do' escaped from me; but I remembered that I was there only to pass the time and to give Morelli an excuse for keeping me company.

'Wouldn't you like to furnish a house of your own?' Morelli asked.

'Yes . . . If a certain Clelia some day gets one for me . . .'

He enjoyed his rôle, among those crystals and the women who inspected me out of the corners of their eyes; some he said hello to. I thought how many of them must know Momina, Febo, Mariella and the painters. Turin is pretty small.

I asked Morelli if there were any really serious people in that upper crust. He asked, serious about what? 'If they're neck deep in vices,' I said, 'if they gamble away their inheritances, if they're as lazy as they want to be. Up to now I've found only some people a little bespattered or some kids . . .'

'Fact is,' Morelli said, 'that we're younger than the kids . . . They know nothing at all.'

'I mean the old people like you and me . . . Those who have the time and means. Do they at least enjoy their vices? If I didn't have to work I'd have terrible vices. At bottom I'm not at all satisfied with my life . . .'

Morelli, serious, told me that I did have one vice.

'What?'

I had the vice of working, of never taking a holiday. 'You're worse than those industrialist fathers,' he said, 'but at least they built Turin.'

'I haven't got a family and I haven't got moustaches yet,' I said.

Morelli looked around.

'There is one that's really been serious,' I said. 'The Mola girl . . .'

'You think so?' he said dubiously. Then suddenly he became irritated. 'Working for one's family day and night is worth all the time and effort spent. If I had a daughter who played such tricks on me I'd have shut her in a convent long ago . . . Once they knew how to do such things.'

'I believe,' I said, looking around, 'that girls in convents always begin making love together . . .'

'But gentlewomen came out' – Morelli continued his own line of thought – 'ladies, real mistresses of the house. At least they knew how to converse.'

'Not that that's so bad,' I went on. 'Girls always fall in love with the one who's more on her toes . . . But here in Turin they don't even take these things seriously. They are sad and get sick in the stomach.'

'They just talk,' Morelli said.

And us? What were we doing? Really, the only beautiful moments I had in Turin were the evenings when I managed to get into a movie alone or the mornings when I lingered over my coffee behind a café window in Via Roma where no one knew me, and I day-dreamed about opening some sort of shop. My real vice, which Morelli hadn't mentioned, was the pleasure I took in being alone. It's not young girls who are better off in convents, but ourselves. I thought of Mariella's grandmother, who at eighty liked to see people and listen from bed to the rumpus made by others. I thought of Carlotta who had got along in life, and probably died in consequence. All in all, living is really putting up with someone and going to bed with him even if you don't want to. Having money means you can pay for isolation. But then why do leisured people, with all their money, always look for company and a noisy party?

When I was a girl I envied women like Momina, Mariella and the others, I envied them and didn't know what they were. I imagined them free, admired, on top of the world. Thinking it over now I wouldn't change places with any of 'em. Their lives seemed to me stupid, and doubly stupid because they didn't know it. But could they do differently? In their place would I have done differently? Rosetta Mola was ingenuous, yes; but in any case she had taken things seriously. At bottom it was true she had no motive for killing herself; certainly not because of that stupid story of her first love for Momina or for some other mess. She wanted to be alone, wanted to isolate herself from the ruckus and you can't be alone or do anything alone in her world, unless you take yourself out of it completely. Now Momina and the others had already grabbed her up again: we had gone together to fetch her at Montalto. Thinking over that day made me feel bad.

# TWENTY

Rosetta returned, days later. This time too she stopped hesitatingly at the door and Becuccio saw her and said: 'She's not looking for me.'

That morning we were taking photographs to send to Rome and Febo turned the lights in the niches on and off, rearranging the position of a statuette which served as a model. He joked with Rosetta and told her that at Ivrea he had been seduced and deserted by two bad women. Then he talked about photographing us in front of the windows to let them know down in Rome what Turin women are like.

'Mariella ought to be here,' I said.

We ended by talking about the play and Rosetta said that now Nènè was preparing the set. 'That's all she knows how to do,' Febo said.

I asked Rosetta if she painted any more.

'It was just for fun,' she said. 'You can't play all the time.'

'These Turin girls,' Febo said, 'know how to paint, act, play instruments, dance, knit stockings. Some of them never leave off.'

Rosetta looked at me melancholically. Her dress reminded me that there was sun outside, a beautiful March day.

'The only trades you don't leave off,' Rosetta said, 'are the ones you follow to eat. I'd like to have to earn my living making stockings.'

Febo told her that hunger wasn't enough to make you succeed: you had to know your trade like the starving know hunger and practice it like gentlemen.

'Everybody who wants to doesn't die of hunger,' Rosetta said, looking at us with those still eyes, 'and the gentleman is not always the one with money.'

Becuccio stood there listening and the photographer – black bow tie like Loris – rubbed his hands.

I said that we had to hurry up. While they shot the pictures, I took Rosetta upstairs and down and showed her how the shop had turned out. She liked both the curtains and tapestries. We talked about the lighting. They called me to the telephone.

'I'm leaving,' Rosetta said. 'Thanks.'

'We'll see each other again,' I said.

In the evening I saw Momina with some other people – new people, possible future customers – and there was talk of an auto trip, of going to the Riviera some Sunday. 'Let's tell Rosetta too,' Momina said.

'Of course.'

Some days later, Mariella and Rosetta drove up to Via Po, and Mariella, blonde and fresh, shouted from the driver's seat that I should take a ride with them. 'I work mornings,' I said.

'Come and visit us,' she said. 'Grandmother wants to get to know you better.'

I waved to Rosetta and they left.

The next day Rosetta appeared at the door, alone.

'Come in,' I said. 'How are you?'

We walked along under the porticoes, talking, and stopped to look at the copper engravings and the dark leather bindings in Bussola's window.

'It might do for a living-room just the way it is,' I said.

'Do you like books?' Rosetta said, livening up. 'Do you read much?'

'During the war. One didn't know what to do. But now I don't manage at all. I always feel I'm putting my nose into somebody else's business . . .'

Rosetta was amused and looked at me.

' . . . It seems indecent. Like opening other people's letters . . .'

Rosetta, however, had read everything. She had been to the university, she admitted hesitantly; she was almost ashamed.

'How was it Momina studied in Switzerland?' I asked.

Momina was the daughter of nobles who had spent their last penny on bringing her up. Then she had married a great Tuscan landlord, and it was nice that she had never let herself be called baroness. Anyhow, the title was no longer hers. Rosetta knew Neri, her husband; she had been with Momina at Versailles during the very summer that Neri was courting her. It was a beautiful summer for Rosetta too. She had been amused watching Momina torment Neri like a mouse. Four years ago. Poor Neri, he was very elegant and very stupid.

'That's what you want,' I observed.

But after the marriage Neri got his revenge. After all, his grandfather had only been a steward, one of those who go around on horseback, wearing riding boots. Neri had an excuse to stay in the country to look after his lands, and Momina had left him.

'Are you more like Neri or more like Momina?' I asked her.

'What do you mean?'

'Your father's a working man,' I said. 'Do you admire your father?'

'I'm more like Momina,' she said without hesitation, and she smiled.

So we went to the Riviera. This time Mariella came along. We had two cars, two magnificent Studebakers. I was seated between Nènè and Rosetta and some baron drove us, a young man, an ass who didn't know the score but did know about paintings. He drove all the time half-turned around to talk with Nènè about plays with French titles. Momina was in the car ahead, Mariella's, full of people whom I had just met. It was still dark and rain threatened. But everybody swore that weekends on the Riviera are always sunny.

Rosetta scarcely talked. Again I was amazed at Nènè, sculptress or painter or whatever, thick lipped and banged, and her shameless way of laughing like a child. And yet she was thirty at least, very little younger than myself. She was also ingenuous and impulsive and, when Rosetta asked her how Loris was and why he hadn't come too, she became confused and lowered her voice as though caught out. Strange girl – she seemed like a lizard. Probably she really was clever, and anyhow artists are what they are.

But I was sleepy, we had passed the evening at the baron's house, eating and waiting for the girls so we could leave. I drowsed off. We ran into a strong wind in the Apennines, and in the middle of the road through the woods the rain caught us. Then as the day got brighter and brighter the rain thinned out until we were running along the sea in warm air with the windows open, under the last showers. Here the gardens were green and already in flower. I asked Rosetta if she was going to the sea that year. She said no, that she was going back to Montalto.

Our destination was a villa above Noli but someone said: 'Let's go to Sanremo.'

'As for me,' the baron said, 'I'd thought of resting a bit.'

While they talked, we got out in the square at Noli. Momina came up. At that hour, in the first light, the square was deserted, the cafés closed.

'We're early birds again,' Momina said to me. Rosetta, her bag hanging from her shoulder, had her back to the sea as she leaned on the railing and smoked.

'I've never seen the sea at this hour,' Nènè said.

'You never do unless you stay up all night,' Momina said, 'but it's not worth it. This breeze with the smell of flowers is better than the sea.'

We started off again. The baron had won. We took the mountain road and, speeding between stone boundary walls and around dangerous curves, we arrived at the villa, which was like a huge greenhouse among the magnolias.

# TWENTY-ONE

Walking in the garden, Rosetta told us that last year she had wanted to become a nun. We had gone off, she, Momina and I, into a little copse, until we came to a balustrade from which you overlooked the sea.

'But they don't want girls like me,' she said.

'Why not? If you have the money?' Momina said.

Rosetta began to laugh softly and said that the nuns had to be virgins.

Momina said: 'Well, that's a kind of marriage too. All that is required of a bride is that she be dressed in white.'

'It's nice up here,' Rosetta said. 'But tomorrow it won't be so nice. To keep some regard for the world and the people in it, one ought to do without everything. The convent solves the question.'

'And what would you have done all alone? Painted madonnas?' Momina said. 'I wouldn't know how to get through the days . . .'

Rosetta shrugged her shoulders at Momina's allusion. I myself was hardly aware of it. But Mariella and some others were approaching under the magnolias and Momina murmured: 'One day at a time is enough. Let's get through today . . .'

The day was really quite promising, if only there hadn't been the women, sisters and friends of the baron, and their escorts who insisted on making a noise and wore out the tormented old caretakers opening the house, carrying stuff, putting the veranda to rights. Momina injected a bit of order by proposing that they assign us women a bedroom and let us rest an hour.

The villa was splendid, full of solid furniture and armchairs, but all sheeted, even the lamps. The wooden shelves were still lined with wax paper. 'It seems like a medieval castle,' Momina said walking along a corridor. When the coming and going to the bathrooms stopped, I sank down into a cane chair, and Mariella combed her hair at a mirror, Momina had taken off her shoes and thrown herself down on the bed, Nènè and Rosetta chattered at the open window. It reminded me of those movies about American girls who live all together in one room with an older one, quite experienced, who'd act as a wet-nurse to the others. And I thought it was all a fake: the actress who plays the ingenue is the most divorced and best paid. I laughed to myself, and Momina who was smoking said: 'I hope they send us up a drink . . .'

'I don't understand,' Mariella began, 'why Donna Paola dresses like a gypsy, and with earrings . . .'

They spoke for a while about the earrings and the absent women. At a certain point I gave a start: I had dozed off again. I felt the coolness of the room and heard Nènè's aggressive voice exclaim: 'You're nasty, nasty. I don't have to mother anybody.'

'You don't have to, but you do,' Momina said.

Nènè, standing in the middle of the room, shouted stridently: 'Men are babies. We artists are doubly children. If you take that away from us, what's left?'

'What do you want to take away?' Momina said. 'There's nothing one can take away from life; it's already zero. Oh' – and she turned over on the bed – 'you make me sick . . .'

From the window Rosetta said: 'If you like him, Nènè, don't pay attention to what Momina says. She's trying to make you angry . . .'

'Of course,' Mariella said.

'Who are you talking about?' I asked.

'That genius Loris,' Momina said, jumping down from the

bed. 'He won't take a bath unless someone's in love with him
. . . I prefer Fefé.'

Downstairs they rang a gong. 'Let's go,' Momina said.
'Girls into the living-room.'

The custodians had scurried around town to get up a lunch,
which we ate on the veranda. Donna Paola, with her scarlet
gypsy cloak, acted as hostess and apologised because we had
to pass the plates ourselves. We had chianti and liqueurs in
brandy glasses. Mariella gossiped endlessly. Towards the
end of lunch the curtains had to be drawn, the sun beat so on
the panes.

It wasn't yet noon. When we got up they talked about what
to do. Someone said: 'Let's go down to the sea.' Someone
else got lost in the garden. I had a fat homely fellow beside
me who wanted to show me the antiquities of Noli. I dropped
him with an excuse. I escaped to a second floor bedroom and
sat down at the window. I looked at the trees and shrubs,
and smoked.

From the garden rose shouts and voices that I recognised;
they were talking again about going to Sanremo. Suddenly
my door opened; Mariella entered. 'Oh, it's you,' she said.
'Excuse me.' Behind her I caught a glimpse of the baron's
face, which dodged behind her shoulder.

'Do I have to leave?' I said.

Mariella smiled pleasantly at me and closed the door in his
face. 'I was looking for you.' She came up to me. 'The trouble
with these trips is that there's always someone *de trop*,' she
chattered on. 'What I wanted to say, Clelia, was – let's help
poor Rosetta . . . You know how sensitive and intelligent she
is, we were such friends before . . . We've got to make her
forget her morbid thoughts, distract her . . .'

I was wondering how she would face it out. I could still see
the vexed expression on the baron's face.

'You tell her too. I know that you've been seeing one
another . . . She doesn't like to come out with me. Convince
her to come to the tryouts. You just can't keep these girls

together. It's awfully difficult to put something on . . .'

'Perhaps Rosetta's just grown up,' I said, 'and doesn't want to play with dolls any more.'

'No, no,' she said, 'there are little feuds and jealousies . . .'

'She doesn't seem to hold anything against Nènè.'

'It's not that. Ever since Momina came out against the play – Momina too! How silly! – Rosetta won't have anything more to do with it, she's dropped us.'

'I believe,' I said, 'that Rosetta tried to kill herself because she was sick and tired of Momina, of the play, of you, of everybody. Don't you think so?'

Taken aback, she looked at me, flushing. Then she caught hold of herself vivaciously. 'You're exaggerating,' she said. 'Rosetta's an intelligent and sincere girl . . .'

Precisely, I wanted to reply, precisely; but there was a knock at the door. It was Momina.

'We're going to Sanremo,' she announced. Then looking at us with narrowed eyes, she said: 'I'm surprised at you two.'

We didn't get to Sanremo. Nènè began to feel sick and twist around on the seat, moaning. 'It's terrible. I'm dying. Stop.' The first car stopped too.

'It's nothing at all, nothing at all,' the baron said. 'It's just car-sickness. This car always plays these tricks.'

The fat fellow and a woman in the other group were sick too. We made them lean over the low wall and vomit. Nènè was the most tragic, with her circled eyes and disconnected words. They explained to me that these big American cars were so comfortably and easily sprung that they gave you the sensation of rising and sinking in sea-swells.

We had stopped under a rocky overhang at a wide intersection, facing the sea. Rosetta looked at the scene with an irritated air.

'Do you feel well enough to go on?' we asked the three.

# TWENTY-TWO

They didn't, and so Momina and I walked down among the cacti to the beach. Mariella shouted to us to wait for her.

'This is the sea,' Momina said, leaning against a wall.

'Mariella thinks that you go too far with Rosetta,' I told her.

'Do you?' she said coldly.

Mariella, shouting 'Yoo-hoo,' arrived with two or three men.

'Shall we bathe now?' they said.

'No, go collect pebbles,' Momina said, 'but don't put them in your mouths.'

They actually went away. 'Listen,' I said, struck, 'do you see much of Febo?'

'He's a presumptuous, slimy, hairy boor. Satisfied?' She laughed. 'Why? Are you interested in him?'

'No,' I murmured, 'I wanted to know if you like only women.'

'Did that stupid girl say something?'

'No, I'm that stupid girl. I can't understand why Rosetta doesn't get married. It's the only thing she can do. Is she still attached to you?'

Momina examined me a moment there in the sun.

'I don't like women, and neither does Rosetta. That's the truth. If I did like them, don't worry, I wouldn't think twice about it. It's an idea Rosetta's got into her head. It happened three years ago, we were at the seaside like today . . . She came in a room and found me . . . I wasn't alone. It was a bit of horseplay, like at Ivrea. Then she wanted to be daring, but the impression stuck and she considers me . . . something . . . her reflection in a mirror. Do you understand?'

I understood. The story was so absurd that it had to be true. But it was clear she hadn't told me everything.

'Why doesn't she get married?'

'Would that change things?' Momina said. 'She doesn't have to make a position for herself. She knows what a man is . . . And then they keep close watch on her at home.'

Mariella returned with her men. Up above they were calling us. They had decided to drive back to Noli, very slowly. I wasn't sorry they had decided against going to Sanremo, but what would we do in Noli? As for me, I decided that I would sit in the town square and spend the evening that way.

We had left Nènè in the other car; I was seated between Momina and Rosetta, Mariella whispered and plotted up front with the baron, and suddenly he turned around and asked if the car made us sick. Then we were off like the wind.

We passed through Noli without stopping, passed through Spotorno, entered Savona. This was beginning to get dull. I nudged Momina and indicated Mariella pressing up against the baron and said: 'Aren't you beginning to feel sick in the stomach?' When the big car braked, the body bounced back and forth on those springs. They turned around and said: 'Shall we go dancing?'

It was worth while coming to the Riviera. We drove up to a tea-room on a square and the people on the sidewalk stopped at either end of the car as we got out and provided us with a guard of honour. We might have been a variety number.

Once inside, Momina expressed what we were all thinking. 'Look here,' she said to the baron, 'devote yourself to Mariella. I don't feel like dancing today.'

'Neither do I,' Rosetta said.

'Nor I.'

It was a modern place, with lattice partitions and palms.

'We're going to see Savona,' we told them. 'Have a good time.'

We went out into the street, relieved. There wasn't much to see in Savona on Sunday, but a new city always has an effect on you. There was a great sky with several clouds, there was the sea air, we walked along aimlessly. We went into a café and had cakes, looking at the women and the people who looked at us. We got as far as the port where we found ugly red and black ships instead of houses.

'That's the end,' Momina said. 'Everything ends.'

We passed by the fried-fish stalls.

Momina said: 'Your friend Morelli would invite us to have a litre of wine. The trouble is I can't stand it.'

'Can you?' Rosetta asked.

'In Rome you can do this sort of thing,' I said. 'That's the nice thing about Rome.'

'I can stand the wine. I can't always stand Morelli,' Momina said.

We leaned on the wall above the water and lit cigarettes.

'This is the way I used to get my meals,' I said to Rosetta. 'Not in dives like these but in a dairy store. Turin is full of girls who eat that way.'

'It must be rather pleasant,' Rosetta said. 'When I went to school, every morning I used to pass by a dairy store and in the winter when you looked in the window you would see the people holding both hands around their cups to warm their fingers. It must be nice to be inside like that, alone, when it's cold outside.'

I told her that the girls don't always have time to warm their fingers in the morning. You drop your cup and run to the office cursing somebody.

Then Rosetta asked me: 'Do you think girls who work are stupid? Should they sell themselves instead?'

Momina who was looking down at the water said: 'It seems more like a sewer than the sea. Do you suppose they wash their dirty dishes here?'

'Going to an office is selling yourself too,' I replied to Rosetta. 'There are plenty of ways of selling yourself. I don't know which way's the most useless.'

I don't know why I talked like that to her. Especially since I thought just the reverse.

Touched, Rosetta answered: 'I know life is hard . . .'

'Oh drop it,' Momina said. 'All this talk about politics . . . Let's shove along.'

Now we were walking in the middle of the street. Rosetta, reflective, kept glancing at me. Suddenly she said: 'Please don't think that I despise prostitutes. One does anything to keep alive . . . But isn't it simpler to live by working?'

'That's working, too,' I said. 'Don't you believe there's any other reason for it. Everything's all linked up.'

'My notion is that prostitutes are stupid,' Momina said. 'Look at the faces of some of them.'

'It depends on whom you call a prostitute,' Rosetta said. 'You're talking about the faces of the ones who haven't made a success of it.'

'It's all a matter of knowing how to look after yourself,' Momina said.

Finally we got back to the Studebaker in the piazza and our tea-room. Momina said: 'Shall we go in?'

The two were dancing among the palms, holding one another as if they were married. We stood and watched them a while from the bar. Tall Mariella's blonde head rose above the other dancers. There's one of 'em who knows how to look out for herself, I was thinking.

They came up to us, smiling a bit stupidly. They had drunk quite a few. The baron asked Rosetta to dance. They danced. Then we told him it would be best to return. Mariella, excited, told us that she would have liked to have seen Savona with us. Rosetta, very serious, said that she hadn't missed anything.

In an instant we were back in Noli and it wasn't yet evening. The sea began to take on colour. We found the others in the café on the square, bored and noisy. We decided to eat there and then go back in comfort, quietly without further fuss.

# TWENTY-THREE

The next day Nènè, visiting me in Via Po to see the salons, said it was ridiculous her getting sick. She examined the niches and mirrors, the porcelains and frames, prying about; and then she invited me to a little party that they wanted to give in Loris's studio. She asked me why I didn't furnish the shop with something modern. She spoke against Febo. She talked about the young painters of Turin, knowledgeably and cleverly. I replied that I was seeing some projects through and that I had a great deal of work these days.

The same day Mariella sent me a bouquet of white roses with a card: 'Remembrance of an innocent trip.' During dinner in Noli the baroness had asked us all if we had had a good time in Savona. Mariella, too, invited me to an evening at her house: someone was going to read poetry. I replied that I had a lot to do.

Morelli invited himself to dinner at my table. He asked why we didn't eat upstairs in my room. I replied that that wasn't proper even with a girl friend.

Even Maurizio put in an appearance in the form of a long letter in which he wrote that he missed me, that people in Rome were beginning to tease him about his widowhood, and that I should please not return to him married to a Turin football-player and that, in short, I should tell him whether he was to confirm the renting of the villa for that summer. I suddenly realised that I could no longer recall the faces of the people in Rome, and in my memory I often confused Maurizio's with Guido's. But what I didn't confuse were those wild times with Guido, his ill-humours and desires and mine too, and the tranquil resignation I enjoyed with Maurizio. Maurizio was clever, Maurizio was in no hurry. You get these things when finally you can live without them.

I talked about it with Rosetta when she returned to visit me. She appeared in her usual way, at the door, while I was going out. I told her that I had been invited to Loris's party. 'Are you going?' she asked me with a half-smile.

'Nènè wants me to come to her party, Mariella to hers. When I was a girl and ate in the dairy store, such invitations would have driven me wild. But in those days one used to go into the hills instead.'

Rosetta asked what I used to do on Sundays. 'I've already told you. I went into the hills. Or dancing. Or to the movies. Played around with the boys.'

'Did you do that in the hills?'

'We didn't do much.' I looked at her. 'Much less than they do in other circles.'

'Sometimes Loris used to take me to the cafés in the slums,' Rosetta said.

'Where blood flows,' I said. 'Have you ever seen blood flow?'

'Loris played billiards. There was often a floor show. Disgusting women . . .'

'What's your impression of these slums?'

'That they're things got up for show,' Rosetta said. 'The wretchedness of that life doesn't touch us.'

'No, it's not enough just to see those things,' I said. 'I'll bet you got only one thing out of all that experience . . .'

'What?'

'You got to know Loris better.'

Rosetta did something which I didn't expect. She laughed. She laughed in her forced way, but she laughed. She said Nènè was right: men are babies, artists are doubly babies. It didn't take much to know Loris, much less than to get rid of him.

'I don't believe in this nonsense about babies,' I said. 'Men aren't babies. They even grow up without being mothered.'

Rosetta had another unexpected reply. 'They befoul,' she said. 'They befoul like babies.'

'What do you mean, befoul?'

'Whatever they touch. They befoul us, they befoul the bed, the work they do, the words they use . . .'

She spoke with conviction. She wasn't even irritated.

'The only difference is this,' she said, 'babies only befoul themselves.'

'Women don't befoul?' I asked.

She looked at me frankly. 'I know what you're thinking,' she babbled. 'I don't mean that. I'm not a lesbian. I was a girl, that's all. But love in any form is a filthy thing.'

Then I said: 'Momina told me about you two. About that day at the shore when you opened the door and found her with someone. Is that what's so disgusted you?'

'Momina,' Rosetta said, blushing, 'does lots of crazy things. Sometimes she laughs at us; but she agrees with me. She says there is no water that can clean people's bodies. It's life that's dirty. She says everything's wrong . . .'

I was about to ask her what was the sense of living then, and I caught myself just in time. I told her that when I had been in love – and I knew perfectly well how much in love: you know these things – the two of us were crazy, that my lover was a flat incompetent, that he stayed at home sleeping while I ran around Rome working; yet despite all this, it's only by trying to get along with someone else that you learn to be self-sufficient. There was nothing dirty about it, only an innocence – an animal innocence, if you like, but the innocence also of inexperienced people who can't get to know themselves any other way.

'Anything can be dirty, we've got to agree what we mean by the word,' I said. 'Even dreaming at night or riding in a car can be dirty . . . Yesterday Nènè vomited.'

Rosetta listened with a half-smile, more of the lips than of the eyes. It was Momina's smile when she was passing judgement on someone.

'And when you're not in love any more,' she said calmly, as if everything were settled right, 'and you know who you are, what do you do with this knowledge?'

'Life is long,' I said. 'Lovers didn't make the world. Every morning is another day.'

'Momina says the same. But it's sad that it should be so.' She looked at me as a dog looks at one. We hadn't even stopped in front of certain shop windows that I had wanted to see. We had arrived at the hotel.

'Well, come to Loris's party,' she said. 'Mariella's going to take me along too.'

When Momina telephoned me, I told her that Mariella was right: that she, Momina, sometimes went too far with Rosetta. But you should never talk about such things on the phone. I heard Momina's voice harden. I could even see the grimace of annoyance with which she said: 'The same old story.'

I had to explain that I was only talking about their conversations. That it seemed to me that Rosetta was already unhappy enough without having to listen to her, Momina's, outbursts, whether joking or malicious. That it was so important not to touch Rosetta on her sore spot. I talked on and I felt that talking was foolish. Momina didn't even have to show me a polite face, she cleared her throat as she listened.

At the end she said, coldly: 'Finished?'

'Listen, everyone spends the day putting his nose into other people's affairs. I hope it's at least useful. You've heard my say.'

'And that fool Mariella . . .'

'Mariella has nothing to do with it. It's between us.'

'I don't thank you.'

'And who's asking for thanks?'

'I understand.'

Then, as if nothing had happened, we talked about what we would do in the evening.

# TWENTY-FOUR

Every now and then Momina got interested in the shop and asked me if we would have it done in time for a spring opening.

'I'm fed up,' I said, 'discouraged. It's all up to Febo now.'

'But you're working here a lot.'

'With the competition of all those well-decorated windows here in Turin,' I said, 'what else can you do?'

One evening I asked Becuccio if he had a girl. He joked, without saying yes or no. I said that if he wanted to keep me company, to go out somewhere together, I'd let him take me. He joked a little, he didn't trust himself to decide.

'Of course, we go dutch,' I said.

He looked at me with glistening eyes, breathing deeply. He was wearing the windbreaker, the scarf and the leather wrist-band. He touched his chin dubiously with his fingers.

'This evening,' I said. 'Not tomorrow. Immediately.'

'I've got to shave,' he said.

'I'm leaving in half an hour.'

He reappeared punctually. He must have run about God knows where to get some money. His hair glistened and smelled of brillantine.

He said: 'Let's eat and then go to a movie.'

'I go to the movies alone. This evening I want to make the rounds.'

'Then we'll make the rounds.'

He took me to eat in a little Tuscan restaurant in Corso Regina. He said: 'It's dirty but the food's good.'

I said: 'Becuccio, no fooling now, where do you go with your friends?'

'We'll go there afterwards,' he said.

We ate and drank, talking about the store and when the people from Rome would come up for the opening. Becuccio had never seen a dress-show and he asked me if men were admitted too. He complained that his work always finished with the fixtures and before the last coat of white paint. I told him that we would invite him.

'They're putting up another building in the Dora suburb,' he said. 'The supervisor is sending me.'

He told me that during the two years that he had been doing that sort of work he hadn't yet seen a well-arranged room. At the end the contractors were always in a hurry. He advised me to watch out during the last few days.

He poured me out some wine. I put my finger under the neck of the bottle and raised it. I asked him if he wanted to get me drunk.

'No, no,' he replied. 'And anyhow I ought to pay for the wine at least.'

Then he talked about the workers who were putting in the shelves. Becuccio laughed. 'That Royal Palace cabinet-maker. I'd put that monarchist to making shelves.'

At a certain point he butted his cigarette and said he knew why he was out with me this evening.

I looked at him.

'Sure,' he said. 'This is the tip.'

'What tip?'

'Sunday we'll be finished. My part will be finished. And so you're giving me this present.'

I looked at him. He spoke good-humouredly. He laughed with his eyes, self-contented.

'Does it seem like a present?'

'I wish it had happened earlier,' he said. 'But you're clever. You waited till the end.'

My face felt hot. 'Look out, I'm drunk,' I said, 'I've got nothing to lose.'

He touched the bottle. 'There isn't any more.' He called the waitress.

I stopped his hand. 'I really don't want any. Let's go where your friends are.'

We went out into the avenue. He asked me if I really wanted to go there, if I wanted to watch him play billiards.

I said: 'Are you ashamed of me?'

Immediately he took my arm (we had been walking) and said that all women are alike: They say, 'I'll watch you play,' and then they don't like it, they act as if they're at the dentist's, they get bored. 'I wouldn't like to take you there. I wouldn't enjoy you or the billiards. But I can't order you . . .'

'Why? Does your girl order you?'

'Don't they do the same in Rome?' he said. 'Don't you order anyone, Clelia?'

Then I said: 'Make up your mind. Where are we going?'

We went to dance at the Nirvana. No less. Becuccio wanted to celebrate properly. It was a large colonnaded room with a four-piece orchestra. I remembered that I'd stopped in that night with Morelli and Momina. It would be funny to meet someone now, I thought. Becuccio, in his windbreaker, guided me firmly to the tables in the rear. For a moment I imagined what going out with him every evening would be like. We would meet on a corner of Corso Regina and one fine day I would see him roar up on a motorcycle. He would say very proudly: Hold on tight. We'll hit sixty . . . What sort of man would Becuccio be?

We danced, joking about his girl. I said: 'Suppose she found you here dancing with the boss, what would the pair of you do? Who'd do the yelling?'

'Depends on what excuse I could think up,' Becuccio said and winked.

I had made up my mind. I wasn't drunk, but the rancour,

the tiredness and the malice I had felt before had left me, I danced and talked, happy, warm inside. Tomorrow I'd think about things. That music and Becuccio's scarf would do for tonight.

'Did you ever,' I said, 'know girls, even experienced ones, who do it out of anger? Or even girls who don't want to hear of it only because they have it in for men in general? Girls who don't like to feel someone in bed with them?'

Of course I was talking too much. And talking just like Rosetta and what's-her-name. Becuccio had me in his arms, he bent me back, he practically walked on me. He had already whispered once into my ear: 'Do you want to go?'

'Girls have lots of funny ideas,' he replied. 'God knows where they get them. But once in bed they like it.'

'Are you sure?' I said.

He took my arm and we returned to the table. He circled my waist and squeezed me tightly to him.

'No, Becuccio,' I said, without looking at him, continuing my own train of thought, 'I like to be alone too.'

'Do you want to go out?' he asked.

Outside he tried to kiss me in the first doorway. 'Well,' I said, still on that thought, 'I don't want to be unfair to anybody.'

'Let's not be unfair to ourselves,' he said laughing. He tried to kiss me again.

I let him. He nailed me against the wall. I was conscious of the sharp shock of his mouth and the sharp odour of his hair. I didn't open my lips.

'You're young,' I said, my chin on his shoulder. 'You're too young. I don't do this sort of thing in the street.'

For a moment we walked arm in arm, without knowing where we were going. It seemed like those evenings with Guido, when Rome was still just a place on the map, way off south, and I wasn't yet eighteen. It was even the same sort of night, the end of March or September. The only difference was Becuccio wasn't a soldier.

He began squeezing my waist again. I wanted to kiss him. Instead I said: 'What are you thinking?'

He stopped, holding me back by the arm. 'That you're coming along with me,' he said darkly.

'Of course,' I said. 'But it's a present. For tonight only. Remember.'

# TWENTY-FIVE

Becuccio was a communist and he told me he had been in the war. I had asked him if he had been a soldier. 'I was in Germany,' he said. Then I wondered about Carlotta, whether she was still alive and whether she would ever again find herself waking up like me, in a hotel room in Val Salice, with a window looking out on the trees.

'It's good out here; we've even got tram service,' Becuccio said.

He went down to pay, and we didn't have breakfast. The owner, in pyjamas and waistcoat, silently watched us pass out of the door. I was thinking that the really important things always happen where one wouldn't think. A miserable little hotel, a room with a pitcher and washbasin, sheets to get between in the dark. Outside Becuccio smoked in the first rays of the sun.

I went back to my hotel alone. I wasn't tired, I was calm and happy. Becuccio had understood me, he hadn't insisted on coming with me. I was so happy that I almost said to myself: until Sunday I can see him when I like. But I knew that I mustn't do this: I was already bored by his way of taking me by the chin and looking into my eyes.

At the hotel, Mariuccia, who brought breakfast in to me, saw the bed intact and her eyes widened. I wondered what sort of expression she would have had if she had seen me an hour earlier. I told her I wasn't in to anyone and that I wanted to take a bath.

That morning I telephoned Febo at Via Po. He wasn't

there. Becuccio replied. He called me 'Miss' in his usual tone of voice. I left a message about certain things for Febo and I was free. I phoned Momina; she wasn't in. I phoned Mariella: they had gone to a mass for some titled lady, a relative of theirs, dead a few weeks. I knew the church, it was the Crocetta.

I went out and walked very slowly along the avenues, which were putting out their first green, and I thought of the woods of Val Salice. I arrived at the Crocetta as the service closed; the black-bordered announcement of the funeral and the mourning crêpe were still on the door of the church. I read the dead woman's name: she had been a tertiary, almost a nun. A group of girls and older women chattered away beside the open doors of a large black car. A grating in front of the columns at the top of the steps closed off the loggia: someone had told me it was put there to keep out the beggars and had been paid for by a special legacy. On the lower steps, a woman seated by a basket was selling violets.

I don't know why, but I thought I'd go in. Inside, the church was cold, and a sacristan was snuffing the last candles on the altar. I stood beside a pillar. All churches are alike. I breathed the odour of incense and dead flowers. It occurred to me that priests, too, know something about decoration, but they have no trouble with it: it's always the same and people come anyhow.

Two women emerged from the shadows, Rosetta and her mother. We nodded; at the door they put their fingers in the holy water and crossed themselves. The mother wore a fur and a black veil.

Outside, we said hello and Rosetta asked me to accompany them home, just a couple of steps. We spoke in low voices about nothing in particular; the mother complimented me on the shop; she was carrying a small black book. Despite her fur she looked very domestic, and as we talked she was surprised at everything, and sighed. They stopped before the gate of a small ivy-covered villa.

'Come and visit us,' the mother said. 'The house is small, but I'm sure you won't mind.'

Rosetta was silent; then she said she would accompany me to the tram.

Her mother said: 'Don't be late. I leave her in your hands.'

We walked off down the little avenue. I heard about Momina and Mariella. I asked if many people had been there.

'Don't you think,' Rosetta said, 'that doing funerals, baptisms and weddings all in the same way is wrong? Of course, there are people who enjoy weddings, and even births, and want to talk about them, but the dead ought to be left alone. Why keep on tormenting them?'

'Some of them,' I replied, 'wouldn't die happy if they didn't think they'd have a fuss made over them.'

'People who committed suicide used to be buried secretly.'

I didn't reply, I kept on walking. I said suddenly: 'Don't let us torment them too . . .'

When we stopped at the corner, I said: 'Rosetta, do you like your mother?'

'I suppose so,' she faltered.

'Because your mother is tremendously fond of you,' I said. ' . . . Look at the flowers on that tree . . . They look like puffs of white tulle.'

In the afternoon I saw Becuccio. He was atop a ladder, attaching a chandelier and I had to keep my head bent back while I offered suggestions.

I saw Febo and while we were leafing through some photographs in the salon I became aware that Becuccio had entered noiselessly. A wave of blood rose to my face and my knees trembled.

'What is it?' I asked.

But Becuccio, calm, said that there were people asking for me below. It was Morelli with some women who had come to see the work. I put them in Febo's hands and went down to talk with the electricians. The work had reached a point where Madame might arrive any day to let loose the avalanche of the opening. Becuccio, running up and down the stairs, winked at me as if to say: I'll take care of it. Febo, Morelli and the women soon went away, inviting me to tea. I said no, that I had to stay on.

I stayed to test Becuccio. As I walked through the empty rooms, some half-dark, some totally dark, I expected to see him at every step. Instead I found him at the door, putting on his jacket.

'Going home, Becuccio?'

'Oh, here you are,' he said. 'How about a vermouth?'

We went to the café opposite, where we had entered the first day. The cashier looked at me as she had then. Becuccio said that he was sore at Febo because he was talking about changing the position of the wires and breaking the baseboards after having already made them re-do the shelves three times. Becuccio said that when he was a soldier he had known lots of people like Febo: the regular army officers. 'He knows his trade,' he said. 'He damn well has to know it. They knew theirs, too. But I don't like people who waste material . . .'

As I drank the vermouth, I raised my glass a little as a sort of toast, said goodbye with my eyes, and Becuccio wrinkled his forehead and smiled. No, he wasn't a boy.

So that evening I found myself with Momina and Rosetta in the rooms of the gallery where we had planned that trip to Saint Vincent. Somebody was showing some paintings, but it wasn't necessary to look at them. We three remained seated, letting the people drift around us. I seemed to recognise all those faces: they were the same faces you see in hotels and salons and at fashion shows. The paintings meant nothing to them. Involuntarily I thought that socially I must have had the same effect on Rosetta and Momina that Becuccio had on me. People who waste material annoy me too. Rosetta and Momina had begun to talk about music.

# TWENTY-SIX

Momina said that the only nice things about art shows, concerts and plays is that lots of people go to them. 'Imagine being alone in a theatre,' she said. 'Or in a gallery . . .'

'But it's the people who are annoying.'

'Really?' Momina said. 'These concerts and plays aren't always enjoyable. You only go when you want to see people and talk. It's like going visiting . . .'

'Music, no,' Rosetta said. 'You've got to be alone with music. When they used to give passable concerts in Turin . . .'

I wondered what Becuccio would have said. But it was absurd even to think about him. There's nothing like spending a night together on the same pillow to understand that everyone is made differently and has his own road to follow.

I said to Rosetta: 'Do you really like music?'

'I don't like it but it's . . . it's something. Maybe only suffering.'

'It must be like painting,' Momina said.

'Oh, no,' Rosetta said. 'Painting is an ambition. But listening to music you let yourself go . . .'

I smiled slightly to myself. With so many things in the world, with so many things that both of them knew and possessed, they talked about music as if it were cocaine or the first cigarette.

'I believe that artists don't suffer at all,' Momina said. 'They make whoever listens to them feel bad, if he takes them seriously.'

'It's the others who suffer and enjoy,' Rosetta said. 'Always the others.'

I said: 'You mean like bartenders never being drunks?'

'Whores never enjoy it,' Momina said. Rosetta jumped too. 'Do you know anyone who's more a whore than Nènè?' Momina continued. 'She's intelligent, she's got her craft right at her fingertips and all the temperament that a sculptress can possibly have. Why doesn't she just sculpt? Oh no. She has to dress like a little girl, fall in love, get stinko. One fine day she'll find herself pregnant. She's got the face for it . . . She thinks the men fall for her babyishness.'

'You're nasty,' Rosetta said.

'Momina's right,' I cried. 'It's the work you do that counts, not the way you do it.'

'I don't know what counts,' Momina said. She looked at us almost surprised, innocent. 'I'm afraid nothing counts. We're all whores.'

We took Rosetta home in the car and at the gateway she asked me again, embarrassed, to come for tea the next day. She asked Momina too.

When I arrived Momina was already there. Rosetta's mother, in turquoise velvet, was talking with a bored woman who shook hands, examined me from stockings to hair and launched into a complaint about wide-pleated skirts, insisting that somebody or other would soon narrow them. I always tell such people that whoever doesn't accept the style when it comes in wears it a year later when it's gone out. Then Momina began to argue and joke with her, and Rosetta took me to the window and told me to be patient, that the woman was a pest.

The mother's hand certainly wasn't visible in that light and airy living-room. It was separated into two parts by an arch; on our side were the armchairs and occasional tables and on the other a large triple-casemented window and a long glistening table under a chandelier. I asked Rosetta if they had lived here very long. She said no, that her earliest

memories were of the house at Montalto; she was born in
the suburb of San Paolo, near the factory, but the apartment
was probably now either destroyed or sequestered.

'You will want to see the garden,' her mother said.

Rosetta said: 'Another time, it's not in flower yet.'

'Show her the pictures,' her mother said. The pest had
stopped talking about fashion and said that nice things were
made in Turin, too. 'You people don't really have to come up
from Rome,' she said. 'Isn't that so, Rosetta? We know how
to cut and paint too.'

After tea she went away, she had another call to make.
Rosetta's mother sighed, looking at us good-humouredly.
'She means well,' she said. 'It's bad to be left a widow.'

We went to Rosetta's room, which I barely glanced at,
white and blue, with a window at the far end. In the corridor
Rosetta opened a wardrobe to show me a certain dress which
Momina said was badly cut. I caught a glimpse of a blue tulle
hanging up.

I really liked the house. The mother, poor thing, must have
liked it almost as much as she did her daughter. They had a
maid, a little peasant girl, who wore a black dress and a white
apron: the mother didn't let her do anything, she served us
herself. Momina had taken off a shoe and smoked, absorbed,
in an armchair.

After a while the father arrived, he entered looking around,
with his glasses in his hand, his eyelids red. He was iron-grey
– his moustache had had that tint all his life –; he was
stocky, a little tired. But the expression in his eyes resembled
Rosetta's: he looked around impatiently, stubborn.

Momina, sunk down in the armchair, raised a hand, gave
him her impudent smile. Bowing, he murmured something to
me, and glanced at his wife. You saw right away that he was
a man of an old type, not a Morelli. He touched Rosetta's
cheek as he passed by, a caress, and she drew back her head
rapidly.

He said he didn't want to disturb us but that he was glad

to meet me. Wasn't I the person who had come up from Rome to direct this new firm? In the old days Turin used to open branches in Rome. 'Times change,' he said. 'You'll find out that it's not easy to keep a business on its feet in Turin. The war hit us hard here.'

He spoke in bursts, tired but positive. His wife brought him a cup of tea. He said: 'At least you people in Rome are working, aren't you?'

I said yes. He looked around. 'You've got to dress,' he said to us. 'You're right. The world is made for you.'

We were all on our feet now, we watched him holding his cup. Fat and patient in her turquoise velvet his wife waited. I saw that he was just an old man, tolerated, and that only the results of his work meant anything to the women. I also saw that he knew it and was grateful to us for having let him talk.

# TWENTY-SEVEN

Rosetta told me she didn't understand her father.

'I do,' Momina said. 'He's one of those men who used to wear beards. Then one night some woman would cut it off and they would spend the rest of their lives redeeming themselves.'

'However, he had a Rosetta,' I said.

'Probably he didn't know how not to have her.' Momina slowed down, stopped alongside the portico, and none of us moved. 'Anyhow, Rosetta resembles him,' she said. 'Weren't you a good student, Rosetta? I bet your father used to say, "If you were a boy, I'd begin all over again."'

Rosetta, leaning over my shoulder, said: 'Young men are all fools.'

'And the old men, and the old women, and the dead. They're all wrong. Oh, Clelia, teach me how to earn some miserable living and escape to California. They say you never die there.'

I saw Becuccio through the door and signalled him. He crossed under the portico and bent down to the window. While I talked with him, Momina asked Rosetta why we didn't go up into the hills. Becuccio told me that the cases hadn't arrived yet. 'You have time for a drive then,' Momina said.

We started off again. I saw Rosetta's face in the rear-view mirror. She sat there silent, sulky, stubborn. Sometimes I thought of her as a very young, a little girl, the kind whom you urge on to 'Say thank you,' and they just won't. If you thought about it really, it was terrible having her with us like this and talking like this, terrible but also ridiculous, queer. I tried to remember myself at twenty, at eighteen – as I was when I first started going with Guido. And what I was like even before that, when mother was telling me to believe in nothing and nobody. Poor thing, what had she got for it all? I would have liked to have heard the advice which Rosetta's father and mother gave their only child, so crazy and so alone.

Momina jogged me with her elbow as we were going up Sassi. Just then it struck me that Momina was the real mother, the elder sister, the demanding and evil sister of Rosetta – Momina who threw stones openly, without even trying to hide her hand, who – like me with Becuccio – had nothing further to lose.

'Rosetta,' I said, 'do you have any friends besides Momina?'

'What's a friend?' she said. 'Not even Momina is my friend.'

Momina, absorbed in the curves, said nothing. It occurred to me that every year someone breaks his neck on the Superga road. We were going fast, under the high trees. When the ascent flattened out, we looked down on the hills, the valley, the plain of Turin. I had never been to Superga. I didn't know it was so high. Some evenings from the bridges over the Po you could see its rising black bulk sparkling with lights at the top, like a necklace carelessly thrown on the shoulders of a beautiful woman. But now it was morning, it was cool and an April sun filled the whole sky.

Momina said: 'We can't go any further.' She stopped by a heap of gravel. The radiator was steaming. Then we got out and looked at the hills.

'It's beautiful up here,' Rosetta said.

'The world is beautiful,' Momina said, coming up behind us. 'If only we weren't in it.'

'We are the others, the outsiders,' I said, looking at Rosetta. 'If you can manage to do without them, to keep them at a distance, then even living becomes possible.'

'It's possible up here,' Rosetta said, 'at least for a while,

say as long as the drive up takes. Look at Turin. It's frightening. Down there you have to live among all those people.'

'You damn well don't have to have them in the house,'
Momina said. 'Money's got some use.'

There was a hedge along the road and a heavy mesh fence
behind it; further down there was a little wood and a large
concrete tank, a swimming pool, full of muddy water spotted
with leaves. It seemed abandoned; there was still an iron
ladder for getting in and out.

'Whose villa is this?' Momina said. 'My God, look at the
shape it's in.'

'If I were you,' I said, 'I'd fix up this place and invite
whomever I liked. Evenings I'd drive down to Turin and if I
felt like it I'd pay someone a visit. That's how I would live if
I were you. I'd have lived like that from the time I was a girl.'

'You can do it. Easier than we can,' Rosetta said. 'Perhaps
you would like it.'

'Oh well, you never do these things,' I said. 'You just think
about them, and that's really enough. To keep yourself busy
all day you've got to be on the move. I'm no longer young
enough to live willingly in the country.'

Momina said: 'Seeing that nothing's worth anything, you've
got to have everything.'

'If you didn't have an allowance,' I said, 'you'd demand a
lot less.'

'But I do have it,' Momina cried. 'I do have the allowance.
What can I do about it?'

Rosetta said that even monks in convents renounce everything but their allowance.

'We're all like that,' I said. 'First you eat and then you
pray.'

Momina drove up to a curve which overlooked Turin, we
pushed back the top and sat inside smoking. In the hot
sun there, we were surrounded by the smell of grass and
leather.

'Let's go,' Momina said. 'Let's go and get an aperitif.'

That afternoon I got a telegram saying that they would come up from Rome the next day. The avalanche was beginning. Naturally Febo had gone off on his own business and I couldn't get him on the telephone. I threw myself into it with Becuccio, we found two painters, it was dark when we were still hammering, checking the lights, opening and closing the curtains. The boxes arrived; I dressed and redressed a window, shoeless, like a clerk. At eight Mariella telephoned to remind me of the party at Loris's studio. I told her to go to the devil and went back to arranging the bolts of material, angry because I knew that the work was useless, done for show; the day after, Madame would have it all redone. The agency that was to have sent the clerks telephoned to say that they couldn't send anyone until Monday. This was wasted time too, because the definite hiring was really up to Madame, but she liked to have all the possible employees there under her eye and then keep or discharge the girls according to her own notions. Becuccio docilely ran, telephoned, opened cases, without losing his calm. Finally – the painters had already left – I threw myself down on a box and looked at him desperately.

He said: 'I quit an hour ago. Today's Saturday.'

'You skunk,' I said. 'You too. Go away.'

'Want to have a bite to eat?' he asked.

I shook my head, looking around. Then he slowly lit a cigarette and came and put it in my mouth. Opening the cases he had cut his hand. I told him to go and have it disinfected.

He returned with a package of oranges and bread. We ate seated on the boxes and while we ate we looked around and added up the results. Everything possible had been done, the only thing left was for Febo to take a look at the salons and then we could clean up.

Becuccio said: 'We even have time for a quick trip to Val Salice.'

I looked at him seriously, then I smiled negatively, then I said that such things don't happen twice. He came up to me and took hold of my chin. For a couple of seconds we looked at one another. He let me go and moved off.

Then I said: 'There's an artist giving a party. Those girls are going. Do you want to come along?'

He stared at me for a moment, with a curious expression. He shook his head.

'No, boss,' he said. 'I don't circulate any higher than the middle classes. It's no use.'

He promised to look up Febo next day and send him around to the hotel. He accompanied me to the entry of Loris's house and went away without insisting.

# TWENTY-EIGHT

It was lucky Becuccio didn't come up. In the centre of the room I found a coffin on which they had placed a large daub of a canvas hung with mourning crêpe and surrounded by four lighted candles. They were talking about Paris, and naturally Momina was having her say. I asked what was going on. Nènè, quite poised in her red velvet, told me that Loris was celebrating the death of his second period and that he was going to give a polemic oration. But the noise was loud and Loris was off by himself on the bed, his eyes shut, ruminating and smoking. There was a lot of smoke and some faces I didn't recognise. The old painter who had come with us to Saint Vincent was there, and so was the little libidinous-eyed woman in slipper satin, and Fefé of the ball, and blonde, noisy Mariella. I didn't see Rosetta immediately; then I found her smoking in the embrasure of the window; a short, somewhat hunchbacked man stood in front of her and she was caressing a kitten which she held in her arms.

'How are you?' I said. 'Is it yours?'

'He came in from the roof,' she said. 'Nobody invited him.'

The studio had been cleaned up a bit; bottles and glasses and plates of antipasto and sweets were arranged on a table near the washbowl. Everyone had a glass, either in hand or on the floor. I thought that Nènè must have worked almost as much as I had that day, but that for her it would be all over in the morning.

Voices burst out in drunken exclamations; nearly everybody was already tight. I kept off by myself, I hadn't even said hello to everyone when I entered; I found a drink and a place to sit down and leaned my head back against the wall. Mariella's voice rose over all the others, she was talking about a Paris theatre and a Negro dancer, not Josephine Baker.

'Have something to eat. Help yourselves. Come on, eat something!' Nènè exclaimed, preoccupied.

The young man of the ball came over and lit my cigarette. His little eyes looked at me.

'And your squire?' he said.

'I'm not a horse,' I replied.

He grinned as before. He put his hands in his pockets and stood in front of my chair. 'Too many women here,' he said. 'I wish you were the only one.'

'No, no,' I said. 'You really need to see people. One always learns so much from people.'

'Invite me to your shop. Everybody's talking about it.'

'Of course. Consider yourself a customer already.'

But he was stupid, he didn't know how to continue. He grinned and asked me if I liked cats. I told him I preferred liqueurs. He poured me out a glass, kissed the rim and handed it to me. 'Drink it. Drink it, if you want,' I said. He ended by drinking it.

I listened to the hunched fellow talking with Rosetta. He was just a boy, but he had an old, wrinkled face. He was talking about the Negroes who had deserted towards the end of the war and hidden out down there near Pisa in the pine wood of Tombolo. He was saying to her: 'They were always drunk or hopped up. At night they had orgies and pulled knives. When a girl died they buried her among the pines and hung her pants and brassière on the cross. They went around naked,' he said. 'They were authentic primitives.'

Rosetta stroked the cat and looked me up and down.

'Crazy things happened,' he went on. 'The Americans went after them but didn't succeed in driving them out. They lived in huts made of leaves. Such things never happened after any other war.'

Fefé put in, with his mouth full. 'Shame it's all over' he said. 'While it lasted it was a nice country holiday.'

The hunched fellow looked at him, annoyed.

'Are you shocked?' Rosetta said. 'Were they any different from us? They had courage, more than we had.'

'I understand about the Negroes,' Fefé said then, 'but about the women . . . Living like that in the woods . . .'

'They died like flies,' the hunchback said. 'And the men too.'

'They were killed,' Rosetta said. 'By the cold, by hunger, by shooting. Why were they shot?'

'Why not?' the hunchback said, grinning. 'They robbed. They killed one another. They filled themselves with drugs.'

The cat dropped down off Rosetta's arm. She bent over to pick him up again and said: 'The same things are done in Turin. Which evil is worse?'

They were screaming around the bed. Someone had lit a glass of brandy and was shouting, 'Turn out the lights.' Mariella's voice rose above the girls' uproar. Someone – Momina I believe – really turned out the lights. For a minute there was a confused silence.

I sought Rosetta immediately in the dark. I was reminded of that night in my room when she had turned out the lights. But everyone was saying: 'Oh, it's nice. Leave it like this.' The four candles on the coffin and the little bluish flame which someone had put on the floor made you feel you were in a grotto. They shouted: 'Loris! Speech! Loris!' But Loris didn't move from the bed and Nènè went to shake him and they fought. I saw the two shadows moving on the vaulted ceiling, I heard Loris curse. It seems that only a few of the painters he had invited had come and he said rudely that there was no need making a speech for us. The amusing thing was that everyone took him at his word and they formed into groups again and someone sat on the floor. They began drinking again.

Mariella came over and asked if I was having a good time.

She told me to look at the coffin – how theatrical, how surrealist it was – and she started off again on her acting. Luckily Nènè came after her almost immediately to make her carry around a plate of antipasto.

Rosetta was drinking a great deal, she was upset. Now she was seated in a group at the foot of Loris's bed, and they were telling jokes, pausing between them and cackling. In the candle-light I tried to avoid Nènè's eyes; I had seen that they were swollen, I felt a crisis coming on, her anger rising because the party was coming off badly. The only thing she could do was to get drunk, and before long she would be; but now she was still hoping that someone would arrive and liven things up.

Somebody said something about taking flasks of wine and going out and sitting on the Artillery Monument steps.

'Let's go for a boat-ride,' a girl's voice said.

'Let's go find some women,' a stupid voice burst out.

Such things make you laugh. Even Loris, his pipe between his teeth, laughed from the bed.

'And we'll go find some men,' said a woman's voice.

We had become ugly and got out of gear. Or maybe it was only the effect of Loris's painting which no one looked at. The old painter with the Chinese goatee began. 'At Marseilles,' he said, 'beautiful women go to the port-side brothels and pay for the privilege of hiding behind the curtains.'

I was thinking that I ought to go to bed and that tomorrow would be a big day. Momina said: 'Pay? What for? They do the houses a favour.'

Loris, Fefé, the hunchback and the other men all shouted that it was a good idea to make the women pay. Nènè joined our group. By now we made one large circle, including the cat on Momina's knees. Somebody was feeling my thigh. I told him to stop it.

'Listen,' said a new boy whom I didn't know, 'we can go back over the Po and into Via Calandra. We all know,' he looked at Momina and me with an insolent expression, 'that no woman likes to go down that street. Well, let's the lot of us go together. We'll stay in the café, of course. You can see the customers entering and leaving the cathouses opposite. Everybody agreed?'

# TWENTY-NINE

Nènè begged us to eat and sing and wait in case someone else showed up. She told Loris not to be a pig. She wanted us at least to drink and wait until midnight.

'It is midnight,' someone said. 'Don't you see it's already dark?'

'Afterwards we'll come back,' Mariella said.

'Do we take the cat?' someone asked.

The lights snapped on; everyone was squinting against the brightness as we got ready to go. I lost sight of Rosetta and Momina; I went down with the hunchback and Fefé. The stair-well was an uproar; Loris's voice boomed and echoed. I thought of leaving but Fefé was talking nonsense to me and I didn't see the others on the avenue. In short, I followed them to the café in Via Calandra.

It's not an alley and it reminds you a little of Via Margutta. Momina's car had stopped in front of the dive and inside there was confusion; the people at the bar looked at us hostilely. Of course, we could have been taken for girls from the houses opposite, but at that hour and all together? Out with the customers? That was what I was thinking, but the boys – especially Loris – roared it out. I saw that it was all a joke to amuse the boys and that we women were being made fools of. I couldn't understand Momina's falling for it. But Momina and Rosetta had already sat down at rusted tin-topped tables and we made a circle; Mariella sat down, the painter sat down, Nènè sat down. As each one joined the circle it became harder and harder to understand what we were doing there.

Two little men with moustaches, who had been drinking in the corner were shooed away by the proprietor, and we all gathered near the tubs of privet by the door.

Before, when we had come down the badly lit street, we had passed a little stand with its carbide lamp and a man in a white smock stood behind it selling nougat and chestnut cakes. Far ahead noisy groups of soldiers and young men disappeared suddenly into a doorway, and then Fefé had given a little cough when we came abreast of the door in question. It was wide, with inner doors of glass, semi-dark, and I smelled the mixed odours of piss, carbide and frying which I had smelled outside our house in the evenings when I was a child.

In the dive, Nènè was complaining that she couldn't see the street from where she was sitting. None of us saw the street; there were curtains on the lower half of the windows. If you wanted to see the clients going in and out and thought you might enjoy it, you had to stand at the bar, crane your neck and look out of the door. In short, you had to hump yourself. The hunchback and the elegant boy who had brought us here were laughing together and agreed with Loris that a good investigation of that sort of life could be made only by a woman who had the courage to pursue that occupation. Mariella was on pins and needles. Rosetta was quiet, a bit drunk, her elbow on the table.

The proprietor wanted to know what we were drinking. The place was low-ceilinged, with wood wainscotting and smelled of wine and wet sawdust. Except for our noise and the stupid talk coming from the boys, and especially Loris, it was an ordinary café of quiet people. There was even a girl behind the bar, and a soldier talked to her looking at us out of the corners of his eyes. A place Becuccio might at any moment have entered.

Instead of answering the proprietor, the boys yelled and shouted. Really, I was ashamed. I tried to catch Momina's eye, or Rosetta's, and signal them to come away. But Momina

was shouting something, very excited and annoyed with
Loris. Rosetta didn't answer my glances. Nènè had disappeared.

They talked and argued, they wanted *marsala all 'uovo*,
they said that in such circumstances it was proper to have
*marsala all 'uovo*. The little woman in slipper satin laughed
louder than the boys, she excited them, asked where Nènè
was and whether she had gone across the street. If it had
been possible she would have gone into the doorway opposite
with the boys. She said so. She even eyed the soldier several
times.

I expected what happened after. Nènè returned. The wine
came – red wine, out of the barrel – someone had grappa,
someone anisette, someone Cynar. Loris said: 'Madam' – to
Nènè – 'Madam. Show us the girls. The ones we have with
us are pigs of little value.'

'Look who's talking,' Momina said through clenched teeth.

Laughing and yelling they said we should be tested and
compared and have our points entered on a score-card.
So they started arguing which of us would make the best
prostitute; for gifts both of body and soul, added the hunchback. Mariella came under discussion, and she ended by
becoming heated and taking the score-card seriously. She
nearly fought with Momina. But the old painter said we were
all meritorious, that it was a matter of time and tastes, and
that the criterion should be something else: our prices and
the places where we worked.

Someone tried to suggest theatre and night-club stages.

'No, no,' said the hunchback, 'we're talking about real
whore-house houris.'

They went along like that for a while. At the end the boys'
faces were redder than Mariella's. They couldn't find a place
for Rosetta.

'Kid sister,' they concluded. 'Too innocent.'

But they didn't stop there. 'You've put it on the grounds
of taste,' someone said. Now Fefé was on pins and needles.

Some of the group had already gone to the door and glanced idiotically from us to the street. Momina also got up and went to the door. I heard them laugh and quarrel.

'Look, look!' they said. 'An old man is going in. Now there's a whole party stopping at the door.'

'Rosetta,' I asked her coldly, 'are you really having such a good time?'

Rosetta's eyes were more sunken than ever and she looked at me with a vague smile. Nènè, slapping her neighbour's hands, suddenly hit him hard. Rosetta planted her elbows on the table and said: 'Tomorrow's another day, isn't it?'

Momina returned from the door. 'Those fools,' she said. 'Those utter idiots. They've gone in.'

Loris, the hunchback and another boy had gone in. They told Nènè. She shrugged her shoulders, emptied her glass and took out a pencil. She wrote 'pig' on the table. She looked at us, cynical, supplicating, drunk.

This time Mariella accompanied her to the toilet and I told Fefé and the painter, who smiled good-naturedly, to pay the bill. Then we got into the car with Momina and Rosetta and left. I got out almost immediately at Porta Nuova.

# THIRTY

The next morning Becuccio brought Febo around to Via Po. It was an empty, useless Sunday, for we spent the whole morning retouching, switching lamps on and off and smoking in the armchairs. Madame had not arrived. The usual story. I invited Febo and Becuccio to lunch at the hotel so I could be quiet and rest. They began to talk politics and Febo said that there's no liberty in Russia. To do what? Becuccio asked. For example, Febo said, to put up a shop like ours and furnish it the way we liked.

Becuccio asked how many people our shop would serve. Febo said that the number of people didn't count since only a small minority has good taste. Becuccio asked if we two who had directed the work had been free to do what we liked. Febo replied that in Italy an artist was still free to do what he liked because the bosses who paid him had to consider the public taste.

'The public means the people,' Becuccio replied, 'and you said the people don't count because only a small minority has good taste. Well then, who decides what's good taste?'

'The cleverest,' Febo said.

Becuccio said he knew that perfectly well and that was just the trouble. It was the last time I talked with him. He remained for a moment after Febo had gone and asked if I was returning to Rome soon. I told him to let me know if he should ever pass through Rome. He didn't ask me my address there. He smiled, held out his hand (he wasn't wearing the leather wrist-band any more), and left.

I remained alone all day; I took a walk around my section of Via della Basilica. Now the little square, the doorways, the tiny shops frightened me less. Porta Palazzo was renamed Piazza della Repubblica. Along the empty alleys and in the courtyards, I saw little girls playing. Towards evening it began to drizzle, a cool rain smelling of grass, and I arrived finally in Piazza Statuto, under the porticoes. I went to the movies.

Madame arrived at night by car, with her husband and everyone. They always do that. The telephone woke me, I thought it was Morelli, they upset the whole hotel, I had to get dressed and have coffee with them and hear about the storm they passed through on the Apennines. I went back to bed when it was dawn; I was happy because I didn't have any more responsibility.

They stayed on the next floor in the same hotel, and I didn't have another moment of peace. At mealtimes, in Via Po, in the car, I was always with someone. The furnishings did not displease Madame; she pointed out that the wall side of the stairs lacked handrails, and once she mentioned moving the shop to Via Roma. Then she went off to Paris with two designers and left word for me and her husband to get the opening ready for Easter. I spent the days telephoning and seeing mannequins, studying programmes, acting as secretary and head of the business. Morelli showed up again, and also certain women who wanted discounts, favours, jobs for homely daughters and acquaintances. There was a dance in the hotel at which I saw Momina and Mariella again.

Then Madame returned from Paris, with some creations and with Febo. That damned nuisance had gone to Paris on his own account and had been charming and won her over and convinced her to put on a musical review to present the new creations. Soon you began to see musicians and impresarios at the hotel and at Via Po; it wasn't like Turin any more; luckily these things never got very far, for the next day somebody would think of something different to do;

I stopped bothering myself about it and spent the days in the shop.

One day I said: 'I wonder how Rosetta is?' and I telephoned Momina.

'I'll come see you,' she replied. 'I don't know what to say. The fool went and killed herself again.'

I waited for the green car with my heart in my throat. When I saw it at the sidewalk, I left the store and Momina threw open the door, crossed under the portico and said: 'What a lot of rushing around I've been doing.'

She was as elegant as ever, wearing a feathered beret. We went up to one of the salons.

'She wasn't home yesterday. Half an hour ago I phoned and the maid told me that she had gone on a trip with me.'

There was no mistake. Neither Nènè nor Mariella had seen her. Momina didn't have the courage to telephone Rosetta's mother. 'I was still hoping that maybe I'd find her with you,' she murmured with a faint smile.

I said it was her fault; that even if Rosetta hadn't killed herself it was her fault. I told her I don't know what. I was sure I was right and could hold my own against her. I insulted her as if she were my sister. Momina stared at the rug without trying to defend herself. 'I'm annoyed that they thought she was with me,' she said.

We telephoned Rosetta's mother. She wasn't at home. Then we drove around to all the shops and churches she might have gone to. We went back to the villa, where I intended telephoning her father. But it wasn't necessary. While I was getting out of the car, I saw her mother approaching, fat and black, under the trees along the avenue.

All that day we stayed with the two shouting, distracted parents, telephoning, waiting, running to the door. I must have been deaf and blind; I recalled Rosetta's words and looks, and I knew I had known this would happen, known it all along, and had never paid any attention to it. But then

I said to myself, Could anyone have stopped her? And I continued. She just went off like you with Becuccio; and I remembered the faces she used to make, the words she said, the way she looked at one.

Then people began to come. Everybody said: 'They'll find her. It's just a question of time.' Mariella came with her mother; acquaintances and relatives showed up; someone came from the police. With all the people milling about under the large chandelier in that airy living-room, it seemed more like a reception than anything else. People asked how was it that someone like Rosetta who needs to live so much wants to die. Someone said suicide ought to be forbidden.

Momina talked to everybody, mordantly but courteously. And in the middle of all that someone spoke to me about my work and asked about the opening of the shop. People off in corners began to air their notions about Rosetta's story. I couldn't stay any longer. Madame was waiting for me.

The mother's distressed eyes and the father's bewildered, ferocious face stayed in my mind all evening; I couldn't help thinking how much he resembled Rosetta. Momina was supposed to telephone me but didn't. I was in conference with the designers and Febo, but I got up and telephoned.

The maid was crying; she said that Rosetta had been found. Dead. In a rented room in Via Napione. Mariella came to the telephone. She told me in a broken voice that there was no doubt about it. Momina and the others had gone and identified her. She, Mariella, no, she couldn't have, she'd have gone crazy. They had brought Rosetta home. She had poisoned herself again.

At midnight I heard the rest of the story. Momina stopped in at the hotel and told me that they had laid Rosetta out on the bed at home. She didn't even seem dead. Only a swelling around the lips, as if she were being sulky. The curious thing was she had rented an artist's studio and had had an armchair brought there, nothing else, and she had died in front of the window which looked out on Superga. A cat had given her away – he was in the room with her, and the next day he miaowed and scratched so at the door that someone came and opened it.

Current and forthcoming titles from Sceptre

CESARE PAVESE

**THE MOON AND THE BONFIRE**
**THE DEVIL IN THE HILLS**

NATALYA LOWNDES

**CHEKAGO**
**ANGEL IN THE SUN**

AIDAN MATHEWS

**ADVENTURES IN A BATHYSCOPE**

GEOFF NICHOLSON

**THE KNOT GARDEN**

BOOKS OF DISTINCTION